Grave Discovery

Slowly, carefully, he lifted the coffin lid.

Scully was looking over his shoulder as the lid came up.

"Uggh." She couldn't stop the sound from coming out of her throat. She couldn't stop her skin from going clammy with cold sweat.

It didn't make her feel better to see Mulder's expression.

It was a look of absolute bliss, as if he had stumbled on heaven on earth.

The figure in the coffin lay on moldy white satin. It was the size of a small child. Its big head was shaped like a football. Its skin looked like shriveled brown leather.

"Is it—human?" gasped Scully. She was not sure she wanted to find out.

THE (X) FILES™

X MARKS THE SPOT

A novel by **Les Martin**

based on the television series
The X-Files created by **Chris Carter**
based on the teleplay
written by **Chris Carter**

📖 **HarperTrophy**
A Division of HarperCollinsPublishers

To Stephanie,
Keeper of the X-Files

X MARKS THE SPOT

Chapter ONE

The young woman ran through the dark woods. Her feet were bare. They stumbled on stones, slid on slick fallen leaves. Her nightgown left her arms exposed. Branches and thorns tore at her flesh. But still she ran. Her face told why. It had the look of a hunted animal.

Sweat beaded on her skin. Her breath came in gasps. Tears filled her eyes. Then her eyes opened wide as she felt herself falling.

She had tripped over a jutting root. She fell in a clearing on her hands and knees. She stayed there, panting. She was too tired to get to her feet.

She knew the chase was over. She could only wait.

A moment later, it was over.

A whirlwind of dust and leaves rose from the forest floor. Faster and faster the dust devil swirled around her. Flying grit stung her skin like a million bees. Her eyes blinked desperately. Then they blurred in an explosion of blinding white light.

The unearthly white light flooded the clearing. With it came a high-pitched humming. The girl put her hands to her ears. But the sound cut through like the whine of a high-speed saw. Then it grew even worse, with clanging like pounding heavy metal.

The girl's whole body tensed, bracing itself for what was to come.

A figure emerged from the white light. Only its outlines showed. The light grew even brighter. And everything—the figure, the girl, the clearing, the forest, the night—vanished in it.

Only the girl's voice remained. It screamed out a word. Perhaps a name. There was no way of telling. Pain had shredded the sound.

The echoes of her scream died. The light faded. The dark woods were silent as a grave. Then birds began chirping. Leaves rustled in the wind. Life resumed, leaving the girl behind for the living to find.

They found her the next day. A quail hunter spotted the body in the first light of dawn. He drove full speed to town with the news. By the time the morning sun turned the Oregon sky deep blue, the law was on the scene.

"I'd put the time of death eight to twelve hours ago," the town coroner told the chief police detective. They stood looking down at the dead girl, who was lying facedown. Beside her knelt the coroner's two assistants.

"And the cause?" the detective asked. He was a big, powerful man. But right now, his broad shoulders slumped.

The coroner cleared his throat before answering. "No visible cause. Just a few scrapes and bruises. But no sign of a beating or a physical assault. All we have is this."

The coroner bent toward the girl. He lifted the hem of her nightgown. He exposed two red marks on her lower back. They were welts the size of dimes.

The detective looked at them, then traded looks with the coroner. There was no surprise in either man's eyes. Only grim recognition.

The detective's jaw clenched. He couldn't put off the next step any longer.

"Turn her over," he said.

The assistants turned the stiffened body of the girl onto her back. Leaves and soil clung to her face. Dried blood ran like brown paint from her nose. But the detective had no trouble seeing who she was. It was just hard for him to get the words out.

"Karen Swenson," he said.

"Is that a positive identification?" one assistant asked.

"She went to high school with my son," the detective said.

Without another word, the detective straightened

up. He turned and started walking toward his four-wheel-drive truck.

"The Class of '89, Detective?" the coroner called after him.

The detective made no reply. He only walked faster.

That didn't stop the coronor from shouting after him, "It's happening again, isn't it?"

His words weren't a teasing question.

They were a terrifying answer.

Chapter TWO

Dana Scully stood looking down at a corpse. It wasn't the corpse of a woman, though. It was the corpse of a pale young man.

Her face showed no emotion. She might have been looking at an eggplant. It was just part of a day's work.

Scully was a beautiful young woman. But that was not why she had her job. She had it because of her brains. She was smart as a whip and not afraid to show it. She was the kind of agent the F.B.I. was looking for when she came looking for a job.

Her latest job in the F.B.I. was teaching a class in its Training Academy. Today she was using a corpse to show how to spot death by electrocution. She spoke clearly. But she also moved along fast, with technical terms flying like sparks from a train wheel. If her students didn't follow her, tough luck. They wouldn't make good F.B.I. agents, anyway.

"Electrocution disrupts the heartbeat and most of the autonomic systems. Death occurs from tissue damage, in the heart itself, and in the sinus and arterioventricular nodes. We all conduct electricity in different degrees. While I may survive a lightning

5

strike, others might die from putting their finger in a light socket. In the same way, a cattle prod can kill. In an investigation, you would be looking for a round reddish bruise. . . ."

Scully paused. Another agent had entered the classroom. Her smooth brow furrowed. She didn't like anyone interrupting her class. But she forgot her anger when she read the note the agent handed her.

"Your attendance is required in Washington at 1600 hours sharp. Contact Special Agent Jones."

Scully might have a mind of her own. But she also obeyed orders. That was what made her the kind of agent the F.B.I. liked best.

At four in the afternoon sharp, Scully was at F.B.I. headquarters. She flashed the receptionist her badge. "I have a meeting with—"

"Agent Scully," a deep voice behind her said.

She turned to face a large, impressive man. He looked to be in his 50s. She had never seen him before. But she sensed who he was.

"Jones," he said. "Follow me. We're late."

He led her down a long empty hallway. Their footsteps echoed on the cold marble floor. Scully had to half run to keep up with his long-legged stride.

"Am I in some kind of trouble?" she asked.

"You're being interviewed," Jones said, "at a very high level."

Jones ushered her through a set of large double doors. Inside was a conference room. Six men sat around an oval table. They were in their 60s. Scully didn't have to know their titles to feel their power. It flowed out of them like the chill from an open freezer door.

Jones showed Scully to a chair. He remained standing behind her.

The man who spoke first looked to be the oldest one there. But age had not dimmed his gaze. Scully could feel it boring into her. And there was nothing feeble in his voice. It was as hard and cold as steel.

"Agent Scully, thank you for coming," the man said. "We see you've been with the Bureau for two years."

"Yes, sir," Scully said.

"You have an undergraduate degree in astronomy," the man went on. "You then graduated medical school. But you chose not to practice. Instead you got an advanced degree in physics. Please explain your different studies."

"Well, sir, I come from a very bookish family," Scully said. "I guess science was my way of rebelling."

Scully saw her little joke fall flat. Not a single smile appeared in the room.

Scully cleared her throat and went on. "After med school, I considered doing research for the National

Space Institute. I thought physics would help me there. But I decided to join the F.B.I. instead. I finished my physics degree at the F.B.I. Academy."

The men at the table leafed through thick folders. Scully knew that her whole life was there in black and white. For long moments, the only sound was rustling paper.

Then a second man suddenly asked, "Are you familiar with an agent named Fox Mulder?"

"Yes, I am," Scully said. The name did ring a distant bell.

"In what way?" the second man asked.

"By reputation," Scully replied. "Other agents sometimes talk about him. At the Academy I heard him called by a nickname. 'Spooky' Mulder."

Jones cut in. "I assure you, that reputation is not accurate. Mulder is a superbly capable agent. He graduated from Harvard and Oxford with honors in psychology. His paper on serial killers and the occult helped us crack one of our toughest cases. He may be the best analyst in the Criminal Division."

That was as far as Jones got. The first man bluntly interrupted him. "Unfortunately, on his own, Agent Mulder has developed a strong interest in a rather odd project. More than a strong interest, in fact. A total obsession. Are you familiar with the so-called X-files?"

"Vaguely, sir," Scully said. "I believe they have to do with strange happenings, unexplained phenomena."

"They're a grab bag of outrageous ghost stories," the second man growled.

The first man gave the speaker a sharp look. Then he turned back to Scully. "Agent Mulder insists on spending his and the Bureau's time investigating cases in these files. He will not listen to suggestions that he take other assignments."

The first man let Scully digest this information. Then he went on, "Ms. Scully, because of your excellent qualifications, you will assist Mulder in investigating the X-files. You will write field reports of these investigations. You will also give your frank opinion of their value. You will submit your reports to this group and this group only."

Scully cased out her assignment instantly. It was a no-brainer.

"Am I to understand you want me to debunk the X-files project, sir?" she asked.

There was a moment of tense silence.

The first man said, "Agent Scully, we trust you'll make a proper scientific analysis. If your reports cast doubt on the X-files, so be it. I'm sure we can use Agent Mulder's great talents elsewhere. And yours of course as well. Your career will flourish— when the X-files are behind you."

His tone was clipped. It cut off further questions.

Scully knew the only thing to say and she said it. "Yes, sir."

"Agent Jones will give you a full briefing," said the first man.

"We look forward to your reports," said the second man. "Your *candid* reports. Don't mince words. You can call a spade a spade—and a nut a nut."

Scully waited until she was out in the corridor with Jones. Then she asked, "So what is Mulder really like?"

Jones pursed his lips, clicked his tongue. "Mulder? Bright. Very bright. Also highly independent. Often difficult. In short, weird by F.B.I. standards." He paused, and added, "he'll know exactly what you're up to."

Scully gave him her best innocent look. "I'm not up to anything, sir. I'm just following orders."

Chapter THREE

Scully expected just one thing when she went to meet Fox Mulder. She expected the unexpected.

She was not disappointed.

Mulder's office was in the basement of F.B.I. Headquarters. His door was unmarked. Without Jones to take her there, Scully never would have found it.

Jones knocked but did not wait for an answer to open the door. Scully followed him inside.

It was not like any other F.B.I. office she had ever seen. Books lined the walls from floor to ceiling. Tables were piled high with old newspapers and stacks of papers and reports. They overflowed onto the floor, along with photos of blurred objects. Scully read a wall poster that said: "I WANT TO BELIEVE."

Mulder was standing at a table when they entered. He was examining a photo slide under an intense light. He reluctantly looked up from it to greet his visitors.

Scully got her first good look at him. Even then it was hard to get a fix on him. It was like trying to put together two parts of a puzzle that didn't seem to fit.

11

His face was young, even boyish, for an F.B.I. agent. His hair was a lot longer than the Bureau liked. He could have landed a job as a veejay on MTV.

Except for his eyes.

There was something old and haunted in his eyes. Something knowing. Something wise.

Mulder gave a crooked smile of welcome. "Sorry," he said, "nobody down here but the F.B.I.'s most unwanted."

Jones replied in a no-nonsense voice, "Mulder, I want you to meet your new assistant. Special Agent Dana Scully, Fox Mulder."

"An assistant? Nice to know I'm suddenly so highly regarded." Mulder turned to Scully. "Who did you tick off to get stuck with this detail, Scully?"

Scully kept her cool. She could already see that Mulder would take all the cool she had—and then some.

"Actually, I'm looking forward to working with you."

"Really?" Mulder said. He looked into her eyes. "I was under the impression you were sent to spy on me."

Scully's polite smile stiffened. "If you doubt my qualifications, I'll be glad to list them for you," she said.

Mulder didn't bother answering. Instead he

rummaged through a stack of papers. Finally he came up with a thick folder.

" 'Einstein's Twin Paradox—A New Interpretation,' " he read. "Dana Scully's master's thesis. Now there's a qualification, rewriting Einstein."

"Did you bother reading it?" Scully asked. She could not keep a touch of ice out of her voice.

"Oh, yes," Mulder said. "I liked it. The trouble is, in most of my work, the laws of physics don't seem to work."

"You should also know that Agent Scully is a doctor of medicine," Jones told him. "She is teaching at the Academy."

"Yes, I know," Mulder said. "Maybe we can get her medical opinion on this."

Mulder flipped off the lights in the room. He turned on his slide projector. He inserted the photo slide he had been looking at. The picture appeared on a wall screen.

Scully saw a dead young woman lying facedown in a forest clearing.

"Oregon female. Age twenty-one. No explainable cause of death. Zip."

He showed a second slide. "Two distinct marks, however, found on her lower back. Can you ID them, Dr. Scully?"

Scully moved closer to the screen. She studied the twin marks.

"Needle punctures, maybe," she said. "An animal bite, perhaps. Or possibly electrocution."

"How's your chemistry?" asked Mulder. "This is the substance found in the surrounding tissue."

Talk about snap quizzes, Scully thought, as she studied the fresh slide. She hadn't had one like this since her first year in college.

She bit her lip, then said, "It's inorganic. But it's not like anything I've seen. Is it some kind of synthetic protein?"

Mulder shrugged. "Beats me. I've never seen it either. But look at this—from Sturgis, South Dakota."

He flashed a new slide. This time the corpse was a big burly male biker. But the marks were the same.

Then yet another slide appeared. A man was lying facedown in the snow. Again the marks were in the same place. "Shamrock, Texas," Mulder said.

"Do you have a theory?" Scully asked.

"Me? I have plenty of theories," Mulder said. "But maybe you have a theory, too. A theory why the Bureau won't listen to me. Why the Bureau labels these cases unexplained phenomena. Why the Bureau thinks they should be filed away and forgotten."

Abruptly Mulder stopped his tirade. He asked Scully the hardest question of the day. "Do you believe in extraterrestrials?"

Scully played for time to come up with a good answer. "I've never exactly given it much thought," she said.

"As a scientist," Mulder pressed her.

"Logically, I'd have to say no." Scully kept her tone hesitant. She had to work with this guy. No sense starting off by rubbing him the wrong way. "The distances from the far reaches of space are too vast. The energy needed alone would exceed a spacecraft's—"

"Spare me your textbook wisdom," Mulder snapped. "That girl in Oregon. She's the fourth member of her graduating high school class to die mysteriously. Science as we know it offers no answers. Don't we have to go beyond it? Don't we have to consider what you'd call 'the fantastic'?"

Scully had gone as far as she could to keep the peace. Pussyfooting wasn't her style. Speaking her mind was.

"If we don't know why the girl died," she said, "It's because something was missed in the autopsy. It must have been a sloppy postmortem. There's only one thing that I accept as fantastic. The notion that there are answers beyond the realm of science. The answers are there. You just have to know where to look."

A smile of delight lit Mulder's face.

"I'm glad you think so, Agent Scully," he said.

"I'm sure Agent Jones here agrees with you. As does everyone else yanking the chain of command. Hey, that's what the 'I' in the F.B.I. stands for. Investigation is our job. And we'd better get started on it right away."

Mulder turned off the slide machine and snapped the lights back on.

"See you bright and early tomorrow morning, Scully," he said cheerfully. "We leave for Oregon at eight A.M. sharp."

Chapter FOUR

The next morning, Scully was on a Boeing 747 flying to Oregon. She sat in a center aisle seat. Beside her, Mulder lay stretched over four seats fast asleep.

Scully had her Walkman on, playing folk-rock. She had a thick file folder on her lap. But she wasn't listening or reading. She knew the songs by heart. And she had already digested the files. They dealt with the strange deaths of four of the Bellefleur High School graduating class of '89. She'd think more about them later. Right now she was thinking about seeing her boyfriend, Ethan Minette, last night.

Ethan had not minded when she broke their weekend date. She knew he wouldn't. All she had to tell him was that she had a job to do. He'd do the same thing to her. In fact, he had many times. Work came first for both of them—and especially for Ethan.

He said he had heard of Mulder, though. A year ago "Spooky" Mulder had convinced an Iowa congressman to fund UFO research. By now it was a

Washington, D.C., joke. Ethan knew all about that kind of thing. His job was bending congressmen's ears, and sometimes their arms, to vote the way his bosses wanted. The job paid well, and Ethan worked at it night and day. He went out with Scully when he happened to be free—if she could fit him into her own crowded schedule. They were spare time sweethearts. The most that Scully could say was that it was better than nothing.

It was easy to stop thinking of Ethan. Out of sight, out of mind. But she couldn't stop remembering her last conversation with Jones.

After leaving Mulder's office, Scully had asked Jones, "Why do they want Mulder so badly?"

"They have their reasons," Jones said.

"And why did they choose me?" Scully asked.

"Actually, *I* chose you," Jones said.

"So why did you choose me?" Scully asked.

"Because I knew you would be—fair," Jones said.

Jones had said nothing more. But the look he gave Scully did. It said that he was counting on Scully to give the Bureau the straight scoop. It also said that he had different ideas about Mulder than did the old men upstairs.

Scully glanced sideways at Mulder. Sleeping, he looked innocent and defenseless as a baby. Was he a genius in trouble or a troublesome nut? She'd have to wait, watch, and see.

Suddenly the seat belt lights flashed on.

The flight captain's voice came over the loud-speaker. "I'd like to ask all passengers to fasten their seatbelts as we begin our descent into—"

That was as far as he got. His voice died as a jolt ran through the plane. It felt like it had been slammed by a gigantic fist. Baggage bins flew open overhead. The cabin lights blinked off. The sound of the jet engines stopped. Shouts and screams of passengers filled the darkened cabin as the plane began to dip.

Don't panic, Scully told herself. She looked down and saw that her hands were holding her armrests in a death grip.

Abruptly the lights came on again. The engines resumed their roar. And Scully saw Mulder open his eyes and give a happy smile.

"This must be the place," he said.

Mulder smiled again when he handed Scully their rental car keys.

"If you didn't like that plane ride," he told her, "you definitely won't like the way I drive."

Scully didn't argue. She got behind the wheel and started the car. It moved along the airport access road and out onto the blacktop highway.

Beside her, Mulder put on a pair of wraparound sunglasses. He clicked on the car radio and fiddled with the dial. After he found a station he liked, he opened up a white paper bag and held it out to her.

"Sunflower seeds?" he offered.

"Nope," Scully said. "Never touch them when I'm driving."

"They're to die for." Mulder grinned. "Pardon the expression."

"I was reading those files," said Scully, keeping her eyes on the road. "You didn't mention that the F.B.I. has already investigated this case."

"The F.B.I. looked into the first three deaths," Mulder acknowledged. "They suspended the investigation. Lack of evidence, they said."

Scully couldn't see his eyes behind his shades. But she had a hunch they had narrowed.

"You obviously think there's a connection between the girl's death and the deaths of her three classmates," Scully said.

"It's a reasonable assumption," said Mulder. "There's only one difference. The girl was the only one with both the strange marks and the unidentified tissue sample."

Scully nodded. She thought of the files she had scanned on the plane. "The girl was also the only one of the group autopsied by a different medical examiner."

Mulder brightened. "Pretty good, Scully. Better than I thought you'd be."

"Or just better than you'd hoped?" Scully said.

"The limitations of science often make for limited scientists," Mulder replied.

"I hope those words taste as good as your sunflower seeds," Scully snapped back.

But Mulder wasn't listening. He was leaning toward the radio.

Elvis had stopped singing. A loud, low humming came out of the radio instead. It was ear-splitting. Overwhelming. Scully had never heard anything like it.

"Stop the car!" Mulder said. "Stop the car!"

Scully slammed on the brakes. The car came to a halt so hard that the trunk popped open.

Instantly Mulder was out the door. He went to the trunk. He grabbed something out of it. Scully's mouth dropped open.

Mulder was holding a can of spray paint.

Bright orange spray paint.

Mulder walked back down the highway about ten yards. There he painted a big orange X on the asphalt.

"What the hell was that about?" Scully asked when Mulder got back in the car.

"Probably nothing," Mulder replied with a shrug. Then he looked at Scully and added, "On the other hand, you never know, do you?"

Scully had to agree with that.

She sure didn't know what was going on around her. She had no idea what was in Mulder's head. And she didn't have a clue to what was waiting for them down the road.

Chapter FIVE

The roadside sign said in big letters: "WELCOME TO BELLEFLEUR—THE FRIENDLY CITY."

But the local folk had missed the message.

The crowd in front of the town civic center looked ready to throw rocks.

"I was afraid of this," Mulder said.

"What's going on?" asked Scully.

"I faxed the coroner's office," Mulder said. "I told him we were coming."

"That's all?" said Scully. "They have something against the Bureau around here?"

"I also said we'd be taking a look at the other dead class members," Mulder explained.

He didn't have to say more. The crowd said it all when Scully and Mulder got out of the rental car.

"You the F.B.I.?" shouted a middle-aged man. "Stay out of our personal business!"

"What gives you the right?" a woman demanded at the top of her lungs. "Those are our sons and daughters!"

"These people have suffered enough loss, enough grief," said a priest.

A well-dressed man with an air of authority called out, "A man's been convicted of the crimes! He's been tried and sentenced! There's nothing in those graves worth all the pain!"

None of this wiped the calm smile off Mulder's face. Scully was getting a little tired of that smile. It was the smile of someone who knew something that you didn't. In her opinion, it was a smile that asked for trouble.

Mulder kept smiling when a cop blocked their way.

"Agent Mulder," he said. "The papers are for you. The people of Bellefleur have gotten court orders against your action."

Mulder took the papers. He scanned them and shrugged.

"Wait here while I go into the coroner's office," he told Scully.

"Thanks a lot," she said to his back as he went inside the building. Scully was left to listen to the crowd. She now knew what umpires felt like when they called the home team out.

Mulder's meeting with the coroner wasn't much better. More low-key, maybe. But no more friendly.

"Mr. Truit?" Mulder said.

"Yes, sir. That's me," the coroner said. His voice was cold, his eyes were icy. Beside him, his two assistants looked at Mulder just as coldly.

"I'm Special Agent Mulder, F.B.I.," Mulder said. "We spoke on the phone. How soon can we get to work?"

"Well now, because of those court orders, there's not much we can rightly do," Truit said. He looked like a cat who had swallowed several canaries.

"Gotcha," Mulder said. "But I'm going to need access to an autopsy room. And whoever does your lab work."

"Maybe I should make myself clear," Truit said. "This may be just a little hick town. But we go by the law. I surely wish we could help you. But there you are."

"Good news," Mulder said. "You can help me. There are three cases we're interested in. But there are only two court orders. We're missing someone, right?"

Truit stayed silent.

"I'm F.B.I.," Mulder reminded him. "I represent the law."

"That'd be Ray Soames," the coroner said reluctantly.

"Why didn't his family go to court to stop us from digging up his body?" asked Mulder.

"'Cause Ray Soames's family up and disappeared three years ago," said Truit.

"Disappeared? Just like that?" demanded Mulder.

But Mulder had gotten all he was going to get

out of Truit. The coroner's lips were pressed together tight. That was okay with Mulder. He had what he needed to start work. A name. Ray Soames. He said a cheerful good-bye. Truit and his assistants didn't answer.

"Crowd give you trouble?" Mulder asked Scully when he reached her outside.

"Trouble? Oh no. Just a little small town hospitality—at the top of their lungs," Scully said. "So, do you always blow into town like the Prince of Darkness?"

"My style bothers you?" Mulder asked mildly as he headed for the rental car.

"We came down here to investigate a possible murder," Scully said sharply. "How can we hope to get any cooperation from the locals?"

The irritating smile was back on Mulder's face. "What did you expect, Scully?" he said. "Marching bands and a parade? The F.B.I. failed to turn up anything using your Academy approach. You don't like my methods, you can always cut out and file your report blasting me. Isn't that what you were sent to do?"

"I'm here to help you do a job," Scully snapped back.

"Really?" Mulder said, raising his eyebrows. "Really and truly?"

Scully was saved from having to come up with a good answer when a big, red-faced man stormed up to them.

"Who do you people think you're dealing with here?" he raged.

"All depends," said Mulder. "Who are you?"

"Dr. Jay Nemman," the man announced.

"The county medical examiner," Mulder said. Scully had to admit, Mulder did do his homework.

"That's right," the doctor huffed. "Are you accusing me of missing something in those kids' autopsies?"

"No, sir," Mulder assured him. "We're running a separate investigation. Don't mean to step on any toes."

"Yeah," Nemman said suspiciously. "Just remember, I'm doing any examinations you plan of those bodies. This is my county."

"How come you didn't do the last one, Karen Swenson?" Mulder asked.

"I was on vacation and—" Nemman started.

"Sorry," Mulder said flatly. "This is a federal matter now. Dr. Scully will be conducting any post-mortem examinations."

"Listen," snarled the doctor. "If you think you're going to make those parents relive their worst nightmares—"

With that he shoved Mulder hard against the rental car. He raised his big, hamlike fist.

Scully didn't know if Mulder was any good at karate. But she was. She tensed to make her move—then relaxed.

"Daddy, quit it!" a young woman's voice pleaded. "Please! Let's just go home!"

The voice came from a car parked down the street from the rental car. The young woman in the front seat had a pale face and wild hair. Her eyes had a shadowed look. They seemed haunted by the same dark fear that was in her voice.

Dr. Nemman kept glaring at Mulder. But he walked backward to his car. He climbed in. The car burned rubber as it roared away.

"Nice guy," Mulder said. "Nice tan. Lovely daughter."

He opened the door of the rental car. "Coming to the cemetery, Scully?"

"Yeah," Scully said. "I want to make sure we're not digging our own graves."

Chapter SIX

Truit wasn't exactly eager to dig up Ray Soames' grave. Mulder had to flex all his F.B.I. muscle to make the coroner give the order.

Truit and his assistants huddled with a couple of local cops as a gravedigger went to work. Sweat rolled off the man as he dug. The Oregon sun was hot. The noontime air was humid. The Bellefleur Hillside Cemetery felt like a steambath.

Mulder, though, stayed cool as ever. He munched on sunflower seeds as he watched the black dirt fly. He looked like a cow munching cud, thought Scully. She felt her blouse dampen under the armpits.

"This is a waste of time—and sweat," she griped. "What about this Danny Doty we've heard about? He was convicted of one of the killings. He could have done them all."

"Danny Doty turned himself in," Mulder said. "He said he killed all three. Trouble was, the cops could connect him to just one. Even then, they didn't have much on him. A tiny bit of evidence, and a lot of guesswork. Without his confession, he would have walked free. But everybody was so eager to find a killer, they took his word as gospel. The locals like to think Danny killed the others, too—just so they can put it all behind them."

"So you say," Scully protested. "But why would he confess to murders he didn't do?"

"Happens all the time. Some folks just like to call themselves killers," said Mulder. He munched on a sunflower seed and spit out the husk. "Anyway, Danny's in a prison sixty miles north of here. We can go ask him."

"And get what for an answer?" Scully grimaced. "More stuff you won't believe? Maybe he'll confess to the latest murder, too. He'll say he slipped between the bars and did it."

"Never underestimate what a man doing life will say," said Mulder.

Scully watched the coffin being hoisted out of the open grave. "It'll be more than we get from this guy here," she commented grimly.

The grave didn't want to give the coffin up, though. Roots had wrapped around it underground. The strap from the hoist strained to break that stranglehold. Scully found herself holding her breath as the coffin lifted into the air. And she froze with everyone else when the strap snapped.

The coffin dropped and hit the ground. It started

to slide downhill. A moss-covered headstone stopped it.

Mulder headed for it, with Scully close behind. The coroner and his assistants were at their heels.

The lid was knocked partly open. Mulder eagerly reached down to lift it all the way up.

Scully leaned forward to get a good look. She was a pro, and this was part of her job. As far as Scully was concerned, anyone with a weak stomach should be in a different line of work.

"Stop," Truit commanded. "This isn't official procedure."

"Uh-huh. Right. I'll check it out in the rule book before I go to bed tonight," said Mulder.

Slowly, carefully, he lifted the coffin lid.

Scully was looking over his shoulder as the lid came up.

"Uggh." She couldn't stop the sound from coming out of her throat. She couldn't stop her skin from going clammy with cold sweat.

It didn't make her feel better to see Mulder's expression.

It was a look of absolute bliss, as if he had stumbled into heaven on earth.

"I guess Ray Soames didn't make the varsity basketball team," he said.

The figure in the coffin lay on moldy white satin.

It was the size of a small child. Its big head was shaped like a football. Its skin looked like shriveled brown leather.

"Is it—human?" gasped Scully. She was not sure she wanted to find out.

"I never—" the coroner managed to say, before he realized he had nothing to say.

"Seal it back up," Mulder commanded. "Nobody sees or touches this. Nobody."

But Scully knew that wasn't what Mulder meant.

What Mulder meant was that nobody but himself was going to have the fun of examining this.

With Scully at his side, of course.

The coroner was more than happy to give them a lab room all their own.

He didn't object to Mulder ordering everyone but himself and Scully out of the room.

"It's your baby—and you're welcome to it," Truit told Mulder just before Mulder closed the door in his face.

Mulder locked the door from the inside.

"Let's see what they taught you in medical school," he said to Scully.

"Don't worry," said Scully, "I've examined cadavers before."

"Really?" said Mulder. "Any like this one?"

"A corpse is a corpse," said Scully.

"That's for you to find out, isn't it?" asked Mulder.

"I'll do just that," Scully said shortly. "Just give me time to set up a tape recorder. I want to voice-record my findings."

"For posterity?" asked Mulder. "Or for your report to the big brass?"

"Let's say, for both," said Scully. "And maybe even for you, too, partner."

"Okay," said Mulder. "You do the probing and talking. I'll take the pictures."

He produced a small Polaroid camera. He walked around the corpse, clicking off shots from all angles, as Scully went to work.

"Subject is one hundred fifty-six centimeters long," she said into the tape recorder mike. "It weighs fifty-two pounds. It is in an advanced state of decay. It has large ocular cavities and an oblate cranium. They indicate the corpse is not human."

"Why, Special Agent Scully, what else could it possibly be?" Mulder cut in sarcastically.

Scully kept her voice calm. "It's some kind of mammal. My guess is it's from the ape family. Probably a chimpanzee."

"Try telling that to the townspeople. Or to the Soames family, said Mulder. His eyes danced with pleasure. His camera kept clicking away.

"I want tissue samples and X rays," he added. "Blood typing. Toxicology. And a full genetic workup."

"You're serious?" said Scully, though she knew it was a foolish question.

"What we can't do here we'll order to go," Mulder said.

Scully could take it no longer. "You honestly believe this is some kind of space alien? Look, I guarantee somebody is laughing his head off right now. The same person who switched Ray Soames' body with Bonzo here. We're wasting our time."

She was wasting her breath.

"Can we do those X rays now?" said Mulder.

Scully's voice rose. She was going to make him listen to reason or go hoarse trying.

"Somebody's yanking your chain, Mulder," she told him. "Whoever killed that girl is still running around loose. They could kill again. Easily. At any moment."

"Right you are," said Mulder. "And we'd better stop him right now." Mulder looked at his watch. "It's just after ten. We can strap on our six-guns. Then we can go out stalking a killer that the F.B.I. gave up looking for years ago. That everybody else has, too. On the other hand, we can be wimps. We can do a proper scientific examination of the body here. We can remove any questions about who or what this thing might be."

He paused. His look almost begged Scully to listen to him.

"Look, Scully, I'm not crazy," he said. "I have the same doubts you have. What say you help me settle them?"

Chapter SEVEN

By dawn the next morning, Scully was back in her motel room. Her work wasn't over yet, though. X rays of the mysterious creature were taped to the lampshade. She gave them one more look. Then she opened up her laptop computer. She pushed the "play" button on her tape recorder. Her voice came out loud and clear. She started typing out her report.

"X rays confirm that the creature is a mammal. But they do not explain a small implant in its nasal cavity. This object is gray and metallic. It is four millimeters long. I do not yet know what it is."

Scully stopped typing. She turned the recorder off. She got up to take another look at the object found in the corpse.

The small metal cylinder was now in a glass vial. Scully stared hard at it. But she still had no idea what it was. Maybe Mulder did, but he wasn't talking. And she wasn't asking. She didn't want to hear any more of his ideas right now. Maybe because they were sounding more and more convincing. If she didn't watch out, she'd soon be as nutty as he was.

There was a knock at the door.

It was Mulder.

He was dressed in faded purple running shorts and a white T-shirt. The T-shirt had a small hole on one shoulder. He had a baseball cap marked "Brooklyn Dodgers" on backward. His face wore a sunny smile.

"I'm too wired to go to sleep," he said. "I'm going for a jog. Want to join me?"

"I'll pass," said Scully.

"Figure out what that thing in our friend's nose is yet?" Mulder asked, teasingly.

"No," Scully snapped. "But I'm not losing any sleep over it."

Mulder shrugged and handed Scully a piece of paper. "The motel desk had this for you."

Scully watched him jog away. He moved smoothly, almost as if he were floating. The air was still cool, but she could feel the heat starting to seep in. Already the sky was changing from pale dawn to deep blue. It was going to be another scorcher.

Scully closed the door and looked at the piece of paper. It said that Ethan had called her and asked her to call back.

Scully punched in Ethan's home number in Washington, D. C. He wouldn't be wild about a call this early. But Scully felt like talking to someone who wasn't connected with this case. Someone, anyone, who didn't believe in little invaders from outer space.

Ethan picked up his phone on the first ring.

"Hello?" His voice did not sound happy.

"It's me, Scully," Scully said. "Sorry to wake you."

"I was awake," Ethan grunted. "Somebody called me a few minutes ago, then hung up."

Scully smiled to herself. That had to be Mulder. He was checking her out. He still didn't trust her. Well, he wasn't so wrong about that. She still had a job to do. A job of checking *him* out. A fine pair of partners they were. Each spying on the other.

"Bad way to start the day," she told Ethan.

"You're telling me," Ethan agreed. "What time is it, anyway?"

"Five here," Scully said. "That makes it eight where you are."

"What're you doing getting up so early?" asked Ethan. "The birds loud there or what?"

"I haven't been to bed yet," Scully said. "Up all night working. I got your message and thought it might be something important."

"Nope, just felt like shooting the breeze," Ethan said. Scully heard him yawn.

"Yeah . . . well . . ." Scully said, realizing how little she had to say to him. It was not the first time she had thought that. She had a hunch that Ethan and she did not have a long future together.

"Hey, that guy you're working with must be a slave driver," Ethan said. "What's his name, again. Spooky something?"

"Yeah, that's right, Spooky something," Scully said. The phone was feeling heavy in her hand. She had a growing impulse to hang it up.

"So, you guys find any little green men running around yet?" Ethan asked.

"Well, to tell you the truth—" Scully said, looking at the X rays and the object in the glass vial. But she cut herself short. She could imagine Ethan's reaction. His raised eyebows. His finger tapping his forehead. And she wouldn't be able to blame him either. She would have reacted the same way a couple of days ago. What a difference a couple of days with Mulder made, she thought. A couple of days seeing the world through his eyes. Would she ever see things in the same way again?

"Hey, well, just try not to get slimed, okay?" Ethan said, and yawned again. "And don't let old Spooky work you so hard. Threaten him with the funny farm."

"Well, I'm not so sure that—" Scully began.

"Look, I'd like to talk more, but I have a long day ahead," Ethan said. "Catch you later."

"Yeah, later," Scully said to the buzzing on the phone. Then she hung up herself.

Shaking her head, she went to the X rays again. Why would anything have a little metal implant in its nose? It didn't make sense. And if it did, then almost nothing else she believed made sense.

There was a tapping on the window.

She saw Mulder's happy, sweating face looking through the glass.

She opened the window.

"You should have come with me," Mulder said. "A jog really wakes you up. A cold shower and I'll be all set to really get moving."

Scully groaned. "I'll pass again. I want a *hot* shower—and a nice long nap."

"Aw, come on," Mulder said. "You don't want to miss this. It's the chance of a lifetime. How often can you have a heart-to-heart with a real live mass murderer?"

Chapter EIGHT

Danny Doty was a slight young man. But the prison was taking no chances with him. Handcuffs bound his wrists together. Metal shackles, connected by a short chain, bound his ankles. He could take only half steps when the guards brought him into the interview room.

"You can leave us alone with him," Mulder told the guards.

"We warn you," said one of them, "this guy is dangerous."

"He might not look it," the second one said, "but he's a killer."

"Besides which, he ain't all there," the first one said. "You know, he's not playing with a full deck."

"That's okay," Mulder said. "We can take care of him. We're F.B.I."

The first guard looked doubtfully at Scully.

"Don't worry about her," Mulder told them. "Black belt in karate."

The second guard shrugged. "Okay. It's your funeral—pardon the expression."

The guards left the interview room.

"Actually, it's just a brown belt," Scully told Mulder.

"Who's to know?" Mulder said. "Besides, Danny here won't give us any trouble. Will you, Danny?"

Danny didn't answer. But the gleam in his eyes made Scully's muscles tense. The guards weren't kidding. This guy was definitely around the bend.

Mulder, though, was looking at him like a long lost brother. "Hello, Danny," he said, his voice friendly as could be.

"Hi, folks," Danny chirped like a chipmunk. "Come to see little old me? Not many people do. Danny here's not so popular. Like they locked me up and threw away the key. Like it was file and forget. But that's cool with me. One thing about the slammer. It's safe, man. Safe as the grave. And not near as cold."

There were three chairs in the big white empty room. Mulder and Scully sat side by side. Danny sat down facing them.

"Danny, I'm F.B.I. Agent Mulder and this is—" Mulder began.

"Hey, man, I know why you're here," Danny said. "They popped Karen Swenson."

"You know Karen?" asked Mulder.

"Yeah, sure," Danny said. "She was a good chick. But, hey, it had to happen. Only a matter of time. Bet they did it real nice." He laughed. "One of their special custom jobs."

"Who are 'they'?" Mulder asked, leaning forward.

Danny rolled his eyes so that only the whites showed. Then he stared straight at Mulder.

"Did I say 'they'?" Danny said. "My mistake. Truth is, I did it. From in here. Telepathically. Like, it was no sweat. I just thought, 'Karen, baby, you're dead.' And wooosh, away she went. Don't worry, though. I'm willing to pay for my crime. Another life sentence, please." Danny cackled crazily.

Mulder didn't blink. "What can you tell us about these marks on Karen Swenson's back?" he asked, showing Danny a photo.

"Cleopatra's snakebite," said Danny quickly. "Yes sir, had to have one to be in the club."

"Really?" Mulder said. "What club was that?"

"What club you think, Mr. F.B.I.?" said Danny.

"Was Ray Soames in the club?" Mulder asked.

"Ray Soames?" Danny's brows wrinkled. Then he brightened. "Oh yeah, good ol' Ray. Sure. Ray got a—what-ya-call-it? A family membership."

Again he gave his nutty laugh.

Mulder turned to Scully. "You have any questions for Danny?" he asked.

"No, you keep handling it," Scully said. "I can see Danny and you are soul mates."

Mulder turned back to the prisoner.

"Look, Danny, we want to help you," he said.

"Man, dig it. I don't want no help," Danny said. There was nothing crazy in his voice now. "I'm guilty, hear me? Guilty, guilty, guilty. I don't want out of here. I like those big high walls around me. I can't get out—but nothing can get in. I sure as hell wouldn't want to be in Billy Miles' spot. That's for sure."

"Who's Billy Miles?" asked Mulder.

"Billy?" said Danny. "I thought everybody knew Billy. He's the quarterback. Of course, he ain't calling no plays no more. Not since they put him in the nuthouse."

The State Psychiatric Hospital was on the outskirts of Bellefleur. It was a handsome white building, surrounded by a well-tended green lawn. It looked like a first-rate institution.

The hospital head, Dr. William Glass, seemed first-rate as well. His face was intelligent, his manner polite. His answers were clear. He was one person in Bellefleur who wasn't hostile to an investigation. He seemed eager to help.

"Yes, Billy Miles is a patient here," he told Mulder and Scully. "He's been one for over three years."

"And you're his doctor?" Mulder said.

"I oversee his treatment, yes," Dr. Glass said.

"Billy was in the Class of '89," Mulder said. "You're familiar with what's happened to a lot of those kids?"

Dr. Glass gave a grim nod. "I've seen several of them over the years. Including Danny Doty."

"What did you treat them for?" Mulder asked.

"I'm not free to discuss their cases," Dr. Glass said. "Medical ethics."

Mulder nodded. "Of course. But can't you talk in a general way?"

"I suppose so," the doctor said. "I can tell you that they all suffered from a similiar problem. Post-traumatic stress. A backlash from a terrible shock."

"What kind of shock?"

"I have no idea," the doctor confessed. "I don't think even the kids knew. But one thing is sure. Whatever it was, it shook them from head to toe. It scrambled their brains."

Scully meant to stay out of this quiz. Her job was to watch how Mulder operated. But she couldn't resist asking one question.

"Do you think Danny Doty killed his class-mates?" she asked.

"I leave those things to the police and the courts," Dr. Glass said carefully.

"But surely you have an opinion," Scully said.

"My work is healing the mind," Dr. Glass said. "It isn't putting a body behind bars."

"To heal the mind, did you try hypnosis?" Mulder cut in.

Dr. Glass gave a wry smile. "People here are

suspicious of psychiatry. They'd be up in arms if I tried anything fancy. I have to keep treatments simple. It might not be the best way. But Band-Aids are better than nothing."

"Have you ever treated Dr. Jay Nemman's daughter?" asked Mulder.

Dr. Glass hesitated. "Yes," he said finally. He cleared his throat. "Though not with her parents' knowledge. She came to me by herself. I did my best, but—" He stopped himself. "I'm sorry. As I said, I can't discuss individual cases."

"Not even Billy Miles?" said Mulder.

"Not even Billy Miles," agreed the doctor.

"But you will allow us to ask him a few questions," Mulder persisted.

Dr. Glass raised his brows. "I'm sorry, I thought you knew. Billy Miles is in a strange coma. A waking coma. He's conscious, we think. But he doesn't react to anything. And he hasn't spoken to anyone in years. I'm afraid you'd be wasting your time."

Mulder winced. It was as if he had been slapped in the face. But he recovered fast. "Then can we just take a look at him?" he asked.

The doctor shrugged. "Of course. Though I can't see what good it will do. And I warn you, Billy is not a pleasant sight."

That was an understatement.

☠   ☠   ☠

Billy was sitting up in bed. He was a good-looking young man, clean-cut and well-built.

But he might have been in another world.

Breath came in and out through his slightly open mouth. Every now and then he'd blink. Those were his only signs of life.

"Look at him," the orderly said, shaking his head. "The greatest football player Bellefleur High ever had. Figured to be all-American in college. Then some bozo ran him down out on State Road. A hit-and-run. They never caught the guy. That was nearly four years ago."

"He's been like that ever since?" Scully asked. She felt a little sick. She could handle corpses fine. But a living corpse was another thing.

"Never changes," the orderly said. "A vegetable. If it was me, I'd rather be buried six feet under. His folks visit only once a month now. Only one who cares about him is Peggy O'Dell."

Then the orderly spoke over Scully's shoulder. "Isn't that right, honey?"

Scully turned with Mulder to see a young woman in a wheelchair. She was matchstick thin and pale as a ghost. She didn't give Billy's visitors a glance. She had eyes only for the figure in the bed.

She wheeled herself to Billy's bedside. She picked up a book from her lap.

"She's Billy's girlfriend," said the orderly. He

gave Scully a wink. "Isn't that so, Peggy? Talk to the nice people. They've come to visit Billy, just like you."

The girl's eyes narrowed. Her mouth twitched— but she said nothing.

Mulder asked gently, "Did you go to school with Billy?"

Peggy ignored his question. "Billy wants me to read to him," she said in a tense voice.

Mulder tried again, "Did you know Billy before his accident?"

Peggy's voice grew dreamy. "Everyone knew Billy," she remembered. "He was the most popular boy in school."

"Does he like you to read to him?" Mulder asked her.

"I have to take care of Billy now," Peggy said, still in the same trancelike tone. "We're joined forever." She paused. Then she said in a voice that seemed to bounce off the walls, *"Billy and I have seen the light."*

Chapter NINE

"Billy and I have seen the light!"

Peggy's words sent a shock wave through the room.

Mulder's and Scully's mouths dropped open.

But Billy Miles was hit even harder.

His eyes bulged. His face twitched. Veins stood out on his neck. His Adam's apple bobbed. His lips parted. An animal grunt came out of them, as if he were trying to speak.

Then it was over.

Billy was a vegetable again.

Scully heard Mulder say, "Peggy, I don't want you to be afraid. We're just going to have Dr. Scully take a look at you."

Scully turned to see Peggy's pale face twisted in panic.

"No! Don't want . . . don't want . . ." Peggy cried. Panting with effort, she wheeled herself toward the door.

The orderly grabbed the wheelchair from behind.

"It's okay, honey," he soothed. "It's okay."

Peggy wasn't buying it. She pushed herself out

of the wheelchair. She started crawling away on the floor.

The orderly pushed an emergency button on the wall.

Meanwhile Scully tried to ease Peggy back up into her chair. Peggy wasn't grateful. Her arms flailed wildly as Scully tried to lift her. Mulder came to Scully's aid.

"Thanks. It's like holding an angry cat," Scully said.

Mulder paid no attention to her. He was looking at something else. Scully followed his eyes. She saw what it was.

Peggy's hospital gown had lifted to show her lower back.

Two red welts stood out on her milky skin.

Mulder looked pleased. Very pleased.

As for Scully, she suddenly felt a little dizzy. A little sick. All this was getting harder and harder to digest.

Scully didn't want any more of this nuthouse scene. She wanted out—before she wound up in a straitjacket herself. She brushed past the two male nurses coming to take care of Peggy. She went down the corridor and out the front door. On the green lawn, under the blue sky, she felt better. More like herself again. Sane. In control. She decided to go to the rental car. She wanted to reread the files on this case. She had a hunger for facts. Nice clear cold facts.

She sat in the car and reread the newspaper story on Karen Swenson's death. The headline read: "FOURTH TRAGIC DEATH IN CLASS OF '89." Then the details about discovering Karen Swenson in the forest clearing.

There had to be a sensible explanation for all this, thought Scully. She'd just have to find it.

There was a eerie tapping on the car window.

Scully almost jumped out of her skin.

Then she saw Mulder grinning at her through the glass.

"Very funny," she said, after she rolled down the window.

"Billy said he was sorry he didn't get to say good-bye," Mulder said.

"Ha-ha," Scully said. "Look, Mulder, how did you know that girl was going to have those marks?"

"Girl? What girl?" said Mulder. Then he said, "Oh, you mean the one who looked like Carrie at the prom."

Scully lost the little patience she had left. She was sick of Mulder's games. Especially since he made the rules and rigged the odds.

"Mulder, cut it out," she said. "I want answers. What's going on here? What do you know about those marks? What are they?"

"You want the truth?" Mulder inquired.

"Yes." Scully told him.

"But can you take it?" Mulder wanted to know.

"Try me," said Scully.

"I think these kids have been abducted," said Mulder.

"By who?" asked Scully.

"You mean, by *what*," Mulder corrected.

Scully got out of the car. She stood face to face with Mulder. It was time to have this out with him.

"You really believe in *things* from outer space?" she demanded.

"Look, I'm open to a better explanation," he said. "If you've got one."

"I think you're crazy," Scully told him flatly. "I think those young people were involved in some kind of cult. You know, one of those satanic cults. People, especially when they're young, fall for stuff like that."

"That so?" said Mulder.

"Of course it is," Scully said. "And the forest is the perfect place for weird midnight rites. That's why they found Karen Swenson there in her nightgown. We should go to the forest. There have to be clues there. Candles. Crosses. Something. Anything. Lots of things."

"Good thinking," Mulder said, smiling. "Lucky they put you on my case. I'd be lost without you."

"Funny, funny," Scully said. "Anyway, I say we head for the forest."

"I say so, too," Mulder said. "But after dark. No sense stirring up the locals anymore. They're getting pretty edgy about our poking around. Any problem with that?"

"No problem," Scully said. "I'm a big girl now. I'm not afraid of the dark."

That night, though, she did feel shivers running through her.

She was alone in the forest. She and Mulder had staked out different parts to investigate.

"Come on, girl, chill out," she told herself as she played her flashlight through the trees.

She saw a clearing ahead. She made her way to it, branches brushing her face. She knelt where the grass in the clearing was scorched. She ran her hand over the spot. Her fingers came up covered with gray ash.

She remembered the newspaper story. This must have been where Karen Swenson's body was found.

She heard a low humming sound.

Wind in the trees, she told herself. But she didn't feel a breath of breeze.

The sound grew louder. Scully decided to go find Mulder. She stood up. She turned toward the way she had come.

Bright white light half blinded her.

She heard a clanking noise, like some kind of metal instrument. Or else strange footsteps.

She froze. She found it hard to breathe.

The sound grew louder. It was coming closer.

Then she saw it. The blurred shape of a dark figure in the center of the dazzling light.

"Mulder? That you?" she called.

But she already knew the answer.

It wasn't Mulder that was coming for her.

Chapter TEN

"Fight fire with fire," Scully said to herself—and put her words to action.

She beamed her flashlight into the dazzling light.

"Hey . . . what . . ." a voice said.

She saw who the figure was now.

It was a police detective, holding a shotgun at the ready.

"You're trespassing on private property," he told her.

"We're conducting an investigation," Scully said, after swallowing the lump in her throat. "We're F.B.I."

"I don't care who you are," the detective said. "Get in your car and leave now. Or I'll book you for trespassing."

Suddenly Mulder's voice came from the dark. "This is a crime scene."

Scully swung her flashlight toward the voice. Mulder was standing on the edge of the clearing.

"And I'm the police," the detective said. "Now get in your car and leave."

Mulder looked at the cop's hard eyes. He looked

at the shotgun. He said to Scully, "You heard the man. We have to obey the law."

Scully followed Mulder past the cop's four-wheel-drive truck. She saw the high-power light bar over the driver's cabin. That must have been what had blinded her. The truck's diesel motor must have made the rackety sound she heard. Sure. That was it. With one weird thing after another, her nerves were shot. She had started imagining things. Impossible things. Especially in these creepy woods.

Suddenly she almost jumped out of her skin.

A flash of lightning forked through the sky.

A crack of thunder split the air.

"Let's get out of here," she said to Mulder.

"Sure," said Mulder. They reached their car. Mulder started for the passenger's side.

"You drive," Scully said. "There's some stuff I want to check out."

"If you say so," Mulder said. He put the compass in his hand on the dashboard. He buckled his safety belt. "You'd better buckle yourself in, too," he advised.

Lightning flashed again. Raindrops splattered on the windshield. Mulder clicked on the wipers. They did little good. The rain was coming down in sheets. But that didn't stop Mulder from pressing the accelerator to the floor. The car roared out of the forest and onto the highway.

Meanwhile Scully was examining the scorched earth and ashes she had scooped up in the clearing.

"What do you think caused this?" she asked.

"Brush fire?" said Mulder, deadpan. "Campers?" He grinned. "Why ask me? You know you don't like my ideas."

"It could be some kind of rite. Maybe a sacrifice," said Scully. "I think I was right about a satanic cult. I want to go back there."

"Uh-huh. Sure," Mulder said. He did not seem very interested. Scully might have been talking about the weather. Mulder was paying more attention to finding a good station on the car radio.

His hand froze on a radio push button.

A humming sound came and went on the set, as if they had passed under a power line.

"Look," Mulder said.

Scully followed his gaze to the compass. Its needle was moving for no reason.

Mulder looked out the window.

"You okay, Mulder?" asked Scully. "What are you looking for?"

Mulder didn't answer. He just kept driving through the rain. Pools were forming on the highway. But the car roared along.

"Hey, Mulder, maybe you should—" she started to say.

An awesome flash of lightning cut off her words.

The flash filled the sky. It filled the car with light as well.

Then everything went dark.

The car lights had gone off.

The only sound was the beating rain.

The engine was still.

The car was coasting on the asphalt, slowing down. It came to a stop on the side of the road.

"Wow," Scully said. "What happened?"

"We lost power. Brakes. Steering. Everything," Mulder told her. But he didn't seem bothered. If anything, he sounded pleased. Happy, even. Like a kid who had grabbed a gold ring on a merry-go-round.

He looked at his watch.

"We lost three minutes!" he almost shouted with delight.

"We lost what?" said Scully.

"Three minutes!" Mulder announced again.

Then he was out of the car walking down the highway in the pouring rain. Scully sighed and went out after him. She was as bad as a kid following the Pied Piper, she thought.

Thirty yards up the road, Mulder stopped. He waited for Scully to catch up.

"We lost three minutes of time," he told her again. "I looked at my watch just before the flash. It was three minutes after nine o'clock. Right afterward, it was seven after nine. And right here, look!"

He pointed down at the blacktop. A big orange X shimmered in the rain. Scully tried to remember when Mulder had spray-painted it there. It took her a moment. Only yesterday. It seemed a year ago. So much had happened since. Around them. And inside of her.

This case was getting to be too much, thought Scully. She knew how a computer must feel overloaded with data. And with a power surge to boot.

She wished things would stop happening, for a little while at least.

But they refused to.

"Abductees report strange time loss," said Mulder. "So do people who have made sightings."

Abductees, thought Scully with a grimace. Mulder wouldn't give up on his ideas about space aliens. He really and truly believed that such things existed. That they were out there in the night. Ready to jump.

"Look, you can't tell me that—" Scully began.

"Look!" Mulder said.

He pointed back up the road. The car headlights had flashed back on by themselves.

"What the—" Scully gasped.

"I warned you about my driving," Mulder said.

"No telling what'll happen when I'm at the wheel. You have to be ready to get shaken up."

"I'll tell you what I want to happen right now," Scully said. "I want you to drive us straight back to the hotel. No stops. No detours. No passing go."

"Sure thing," Mulder said. "We've seen enough tonight."

"More than enough," Scully assured him.

She sighed with relief when she was at last back alone in her room. A good hot shower, a good night's sleep, and this would seem like a bad dream.

First, though, she had a job to do. She put her laptop computer on a table, opened it, sat down, and started typing:

"Agent Mulder's report of time loss, due to 'unknown forces,' cannot be supported by this agent. This agent believes it highly unlikely and instead believes . . ."

At that moment, the motel room lights flickered and went off.

Scully's computer screen stayed lit. It was operated by a battery.

Scully looked at her last sentence. "This agent believes it highly unlikely and instead believes . . ." She looked into the darkness around her and bit her lip. She highlighted the sentence and pressed the "delete" key.

She tried to think what she should write. She

gave up. All this was too much. She was more than bone-weary. She was brain-dead. It would be easier to make sense of everything in daylight.

By the light of the computer she found candles in the room. She lit one. Then she yawned and stretched. Mulder would have to go for his morning jog alone again. She was going to sleep as long as she could.

She went into the bathroom with the candle and set it down on the shelf above the sink. Its flickering lit the room, reflecting off the mirror and the white tile walls.

Scully turned on the shower. She checked the water. It was coming out nice and hot. She could hardly wait to get under it.

She stepped out of her clothes, leaving them in a heap.

Then she screamed.

Chapter ELEVEN

Scully held her candle in one hand. Her other hand pounded on Mulder's door.

Mulder's eyes widened when he saw the look on her face.

"What happened, Scully?" he said. "See a ghost?"

Scully tried to keep her voice calm. "Can I come in? I want you to look at something."

Mulder stepped aside. Scully entered his room. It, too, was lit by candlelight.

Scully took a deep breath and took off the bathrobe she had thrown on. Another time she might have been embarrassed. Not now, though. She was too worried to be shy.

Besides, she knew that Mulder didn't have eyes for her. He had eyes for other things.

Scully was wearing just her underwear. She turned her back toward Mulder. With a trembling finger she pointed at her lower back. She wanted Mulder to see what she had seen in the bathroom mirror, when she was about to take her shower.

"What are they?" she asked him.

Mulder knelt down for a closer look.

When he stayed silent, she raised her voice.

"Mulder, *what are they?*"

Mulder stood up. "You mean, those two raised red welts?" he asked.

Scully fought to keep from screaming. Her voice quavered. "Yes, I mean those two raised red welts."

"That's easy," Mulder told her. "Mosquito bites."

"Mosquito bites," said Scully with a gulp.

"I got about twenty of them myself out there in the woods. Look," said Mulder. He started to take off his shirt.

"Don't bother. I believe you," Scully told him. She hastily put her bathrobe back on. She started for the door. But she didn't make it.

A wave of trembling washed over her. She stood there, shaking. Outside the window the rain lashed and the thunder rumbled. Inside the candles flickered madly. She told herself not be be scared. There was nothing to be scared of.

It didn't work.

"You okay?" Mulder asked.

"Yes. Perfectly fine," Scully lied.

"Yeah," said Mulder. "I can see that."

"I tell you, I'm okay," Scully insisted. Then she added, "One thing, though. I'm not sleeping in my room tonight."

"Oh?" said Mulder. "Got something better to do?"

"It's time we talk, Mulder," Scully said. "It's time you tell me the truth."

"The truth?" said Mulder. "What truth do you mean?"

"The truth about what you know," Scully said. "And the truth about how you know it."

"On one condition," said Mulder.

"Which is?" said Scully.

"You're willing to listen to it," Mulder said.

"After today, after tonight, I'm willing to listen to anything," Scully assured him.

"Sit down, then," Mulder said. "Better yet, lie down on the bed. I'll take the chair. You've got a lot to listen to. A lot to learn." He held out a hand to her. "Some sunflower seeds?"

"Don't mind if I do." She munched on the seeds as she listened to Mulder's voice. They tasted good. She should have tried them sooner.

"I was twelve when it happened," Mulder said. "My sister was eight. We slept in the same bedroom. We had since we were babies. The next month, we were supposed to get separate rooms. But we never did. Because she just disappeared from her bed one night. Vanished into thin air."

"How can a little girl just vanish?" asked Scully.

"Nobody knew," Mulder said. His voice sounded as if he were far away. As if he had gone back in time. Back to when he was a kid—a scared, confused kid. "My family had money. They had connections.

We launched a big search. The police. Private detectives. The newspapers. The works."

"And—?" said Scully.

"Nothing," Mulder said. "Then we waited for a ransom note. We would have paid anything. It never came."

"You never found her?" said Scully.

"It tore the family apart," said Mulder. "It took years to put it in the back of our minds. But it never really went away. It was like a wound that wouldn't heal—no matter how many bandages you put on it."

"It's still there, inside of you, isn't it?" said Scully.

"It's still there," Mulder agreed. "I tried to put it behind me. I left home to go to school in England. I thought that might help. It didn't. I couldn't forget my sister. Her disappearance gave me a passion for looking into mysteries. First mysteries of the mind. Then mysteries of crime. I joined the F.B.I. I became their star agent. I was slated for big things. I was going all the way to the top."

"So what happened?" asked Scully.

"One day I stumbled onto the X-files," Mulder said. "Cases so weird that everyone called them ridiculous."

"Everyone but you," said Scully.

"I knew I was supposed to," said Mulder. "But I

couldn't. I couldn't stop myself from believing them. I read every case. Hundreds and hundreds of them. Then I read everything I could find about strange happenings. The occult. Paranormal phenomena. And finally I learned about deep regression hypnosis."

"What exactly is that?" asked Scully. She wanted to make sure she was following him.

"Deep regression hypnosis is hypnosis that opens up closed parts of your mind," Mulder explained. "It lets you remember things you have completely blocked out. Things that are too scary to want to remember."

"And you remembered—what?" asked Scully, half guessing the answer.

"Scully, look at me," Mulder said.

Scully sat up in bed and looked him in the eyes.

"I've never told this to anyone else in the Bureau," said Mulder. "It sounds too crazy. I didn't want to believe it at first myself. I'm trusting you because I think you're like me. You want answers—right?"

"Right," Scully said.

"I was hypnotized by an expert," Mulder said slowly as if he were going into a trance. "I went back in time. I went back to the night my sister disappeared. I saw myself lying in bed, suddenly waking. I saw the bright light outside the room. I saw the dark figure entering."

Mulder's hands had clenched into fists. His voice was filled with pain. "I saw me as a kid frozen with fear. I heard my sister's cries for help. They took her and I didn't make a move to stop them. Listen to me, Scully. This thing exists. I don't know what it is or why it is. But I'm going to figure it out. And I'm going to stop it. Nothing else matters to me. And this is as close as I've ever come to it. You can believe me or not, it doesn't matter."

"I believe you," Scully said.

"But I warn you," Mulder said, "it's dangerous. And the closer we get, the more dangerous it gets."

"I believe that, too," said Scully.

"So maybe you should back off," Mulder suggested.

"So maybe I shouldn't," Scully said. "You forget, I have a report to write. You're not the only one who wants to finish a job."

The phone rang.

Mulder ignored it. "If you say so," he said.

"I say so," Scully said.

The phone rang again.

Mulder picked it up.

Scully saw his mouth tighten as he listened.

"Right," he said into the receiver. "We'll be right there."

He hung up and said to Scully, "It's happened again."

Chapter TWELVE

"Who was on the phone?" Scully asked.

"I don't know. They didn't say. Someone was disguising his or her voice," said Mulder. He was already putting on his jacket.

"What happened?" Scully wanted to know.

"Peggy O'Dell, Billy Miles's girlfriend in the asylum," Mulder said. "She's dead. In the forest at a railroad crossing. That's all the voice would say. I want to find out the rest fast."

"Give me a minute to dress," Scully said.

She raced to her room and put on clothes. She splashed water on her face and ran a brush through her hair. There was no time for makeup. Mulder was waiting for her in the hall.

"Let's get the show on the road," he said impatiently.

"Wait a second, let me lock my door," said Scully.

He stood tapping his foot as she locked and double locked it.

"Locks won't do much," he told her. "Nothing will, not if it wants to get in." Then he said, "Come on. Let's go. I'll flip you to see who drives."

"No way," said Scully. "I'm driving. I feel a lot safer that way."

"You might be right," Mulder agreed. He tossed her the car keys.

They left the motel. It had stopped raining. A brisk breeze was blowing. A full moon in the night sky lit racing white clouds. It shone on rippling puddles in the motel parking lot. Drops of water sparkled on the roof of their rental car.

They climbed in and buckled their seat belts. Scully turned the ignition key and the engine roared to life.

As they pulled out of the lot, Scully told Mulder, "You know, I have a funny feeling. Like someone is watching us. Someone—or something."

Swarms of cops were on the scene when they arrived. Lights from squad cars lit up the forest crossing like a movie set. Scully saw splintered branches and uprooted saplings from the storm. She spied a locomotive and a string of freight cars halted on the tracks.

Mulder headed straight for a pair of cops standing by the tracks.

"What happened?" he demanded. "The details. I want all of them."

One cop squinted at Mulder. "Don't worry, mister. Everything's under control."

"I asked, what happened?" Mulder repeated. "Come on. I don't have all night."

"A young woman was struck by a train," the cop said reluctantly.

"How did she get down here?" Mulder demanded.

The cop started to open his mouth. But before he could speak, his partner said, "Hey, buddy, what's with all the questions? Like who are you to give us the first degree?"

Mulder ignored him. "Was the girl in a wheelchair?"

The first cop scratched his head. "Wheelchair? There was no—"

Mulder felt a hand on his shoulder from behind. He whirled around and stiffened.

It was the police detective who had found them in the forest. The one who had told them to clear out.

The big, beefy man kept his hold on Mulder's shoulder. He squeezed harder.

"I thought I told you to get out of these parts," he snarled.

He let go of Mulder's shoulder. With the butt of his hand, he gave Mulder's chest a hard push.

"And I told you, I want to know what's going on around here," Mulder answered, shoving back just as hard.

"This is the last time I warn you," the detective

said. "One more move like that, and I book you for probable cause. You can find out what's happening in the jailhouse."

He gave Mulder another shove. Mulder's jacket opened.

The first cop's eyes lit up. "Hey, he's carrying heat," the cop exclaimed. He yanked Mulder's pistol from its shoulder holster. He moved fast for someone who looked like an ox in blue.

"I'm F.B.I., you moron," Mulder said, holding out his hand for the gun.

"Yeah, sure," the cop said. He kept the gun.

"I've no time to argue," Mulder said. He turned to the detective. "Look, maybe you'll listen to sense. I saw that girl in a wheelchair just this afternoon. You tell me how she got here without it."

"I'll tell you what I told you before," the detective said. "Butt out, buster."

Scully watched Mulder and the detective facing each other. They looked like stags with their horns locked. Mulder was getting nowhere fast acting macho. It was up to her to do some digging.

She saw a blanket lying by the tracks and gently lifted it. She looked down at the broken body of Peggy O'Dell. Peggy's eyelids were wide open. Her eyes were rolled back so that only the whites showed.

Scully tried not to think about Peggy alive. She

tried not to remember Peggy looking with love at Billy Miles.

Peggy was just another corpse now. Peggy was another job to do.

Scully knelt down for a closer look. A lock of brown hair was clutched in the dead girl's hand. She thought about taking it as evidence. She decided not to. The cops wouldn't like her stealing evidence. That's all they'd need to lock her up with Mulder and throw away the key. She'd just make a mental note of it and type it up in her report later.

Then she saw something else. Peggy was wearing a watch. Maybe it had broken when she was hit. That would tell the time of death.

Scully took hold of Peggy's wrist. It was cold. She turned it over to see the watch face.

A shiver ran through her.

The watch read 9:03.

9:03.

The moment that time had stopped. And vanished.

She'd have to tell Mulder. She'd have to—

"Get to your feet, sister," a voice barked at her. "And come with me."

She looked up. A cop was standing looking down at her. His gun was drawn.

Scully stood up. "Look, officer, you're making a mistake. I was just—"

72

"You were tampering with evidence," the cop said.

"But I tell you—" Scully protested.

"You can tell it to the judge," the cop said. "And you can also tell him what you're doing with *this*."

The cop flipped open Scully's jacket. He plucked her pistol from her shoulder holster.

"Come on, let's go see your pal," the cop said.

Mulder was standing spread-eagled against a squad car. He turned his head when Scully was spread-eagled beside him. He looked angry at the cops' actions, and digusted with their stupidity.

"We'll run an ID," the detective told them. "You check out, you can come pick up your weapons."

"I've got my ID right here," Scully told him.

"Forget it. He's not listening," Mulder said. "He's been watching too much Smokey and the Bandit."

Just then a voice said, "You can let them go. I'll vouch for them."

It was the coroner.

"Truit," Mulder said with relief. "Thank God you got here. Now we can start putting things together."

"Ain't nothing left to put together," Truit told him. "Brace yourself, Mr. F.B.I. 'Fraid you're back to square one."

Chapter THIRTEEN

Mulder grimaced. "Okay, Truit, give me the bad news. I can guess what it is. But you might as well make it official."

"Somebody just trashed our offices down in the civic center," Truit said, shaking his head. "I was afraid something like this was going to happen. Folks around here are law-abiding—but you got them so worked up."

"They trashed your offices," Mulder said. His voice sounded tired, resigned. "But that's not all they did, is it?"

"Ain't that enough?" Truit said. Then he added, "Oh yeah. Almost forgot. Hope you weren't too attached to that dog carcass you dug up. Or whatever that critter was."

"They took it, right?" Mulder said. "Funny how that doesn't surprise me."

"Don't ask me why they wanted it," the coroner said, scratching his head. "Not the kind of thing you'd hang over your fireplace."

"I wouldn't dream of asking you why," said Mulder. "I won't even ask you why you didn't have security."

"Never needed security, before you people started stirring things up," Truit answered. "Outside agitators always cause trouble around here."

Mulder opened his mouth to say something. Then he closed it. A thought had hit him—hit him hard.

"Scully!" he barked. "The car keys! Quick!"

She handed them to him. Before she could ask him why, he was running toward the car. She dashed after him. By the time she slid into the passenger seat, he was already gunning the motor.

"What's the hurry?" she asked, as the car roared down the highway.

"I'm afraid you'll find out soon enough," said Mulder, not taking his eyes off the road.

He was right.

Scully got her first hint of what was coming when she saw a glow in the sky just above the horizon.

"Is that what I think it is?" she asked Mulder.

Mulder didn't answer. His lips were pressed together grimly.

The car went around a bend in the road. She could see straight down the highway. She had a clear view of their motel.

She saw a mass of flames.

Mulder stopped the car by one of the fire engines

parked on the road. He and Scully made their way through the firemen in their gear and motel guests in their pajamas and nightgowns. The two of them stood side by side looking at the blaze. Helplessly they watched the fire licking at their rooms. Streams of water from fire hoses had no more effect than spit.

"There goes my report. Not to mention my laptop. The latest model. I had to pull strings to get it," said Scully. She felt as if she had lost a close friend.

"There go the X rays," Mulder said. "My Polaroids. The whole works. Every trace of what we dug up yesterday. I wonder who wanted it gone. Any ideas, Scully?"

Scully started to say something. Then she stopped herself. "Not really," she said.

"Or maybe you have some—and don't want to admit them," Mulder suggested.

Scully was saved from having to give him an answer.

"Look who's coming," she said, glad for the distraction.

"Dr. Nemman's sweet little daughter," said Mulder, as the figure emerged from the bushes into the light. "She looks like she's had a rough night, too."

Scully agreed. The girl had looked unkempt when they first had seen her in her dad's parked car.

But now she looked like the bride of Frankenstein. Her hair was a wild tangle. Her long nightgown was streaked with dirt and ripped at the hem. Her feet were bare. Her face was streaked with tears. And her voice broke as she begged, "Please, help me. You've got to protect me."

Mulder took off his jacket and put it around the girl's heaving shoulders. "It's cold out tonight," he said. "We don't want you to catch a chill."

Then he said, "Let's go somewhere we can get something warm into you. Then we can talk. Nice and slowly and calmly. Sort everything out. Get everything straight. Make everything normal again. You'd like that, wouldn't you?"

The girl nodded. "Everything normal again. Oh yes, please."

"We passed an all-night diner down the road," Scully suggested. "We can go there."

"I was thinking the same thing," Mulder agreed. "Guess it's true what they say about great minds."

The diner was empty when they entered it. A bored-looking waitress took their order for coffees. She didn't act curious about a girl who looked like a beat-up Raggedy Ann doll. She'd probably worked the graveyard shift so long that nothing could surprise her.

Scully waited until the girl finished her cup of coffee.

"Want some more?" she asked her.

The girl shook her head. "No," she said. "It won't do any good. It won't take this taste out of my mouth."

"What taste?" Mulder asked.

"Like metal," the girl said, grimacing. "Or something. Something worse. Uggh."

Mulder nodded sympathetically. "It must be terrible. You'll have to brush your teeth really well tonight."

He was talking to her slowly, the way you talked to a child. The girl might be in her early twenties, but she had the look of a scared five-year-old.

"Now tell us, what's your name?" he asked.

"Theresa. Theresa Nemman," the girl said.

"What were you doing outside in your nightgown tonight? You don't usually wander in the woods that way, do you?"

"I don't know," Theresa said, shaking her head. "I just found myself out there. That's the way it happens. Always. I'm out there and I don't know how or why."

"So it's happened before?" Scully asked. She spoke softly, soothingly. The girl looked as fragile as crystal. And as skittish as a frightened rabbit.

Theresa's voice seemed to come from far away— from someplace deep inside her. "It's happened ever since the summer I graduated," she said. "It's happened to my friends, too. That's why I want you to protect me. I don't want it to happen to me. I don't want to die like the rest of them. Like Peggy tonight."

Her shoulders started heaving again. Tears ran down her cheeks.

Scully reached across the table to comfort her. She took the girl's hand in hers. The girl's hand felt as cold as Peggy's had been by the railroad tracks.

"You will protect me, won't you?" the girl pleaded between sobs. "Promise me you'll protect me."

"Of course we will," Scully soothed her. "You can be sure of that."

Scully had a bitter taste in her mouth now. A metallic taste.

She knew what it was.

The taste of a lie.

Chapter FOURTEEN

Scully couldn't lie to herself anymore.

She could no longer pretend that this was an ordinary case. She could no longer tell herself that science would give her all the answers. Or that her F.B.I. training would lead her to the killer.

Even worse, she could no longer dismiss Mulder as a loose cannon, a screwball, off the wall, or cuckoo.

She was almost glad that her laptop was trashed. For the time being, she didn't have to worry about writing her report.

It would be tough to convince her F.B.I. bosses that Mulder was onto something. Maybe impossible. She couldn't see them believing it. She wouldn't have believed it—until now. She'd have to watch her step when she wrote up this case. It wouldn't be just Mulder's job on the line. It was her future, too. Not to mention what would happen to the X-files. The Bureau brass would lock those files up and throw away the key.

Scully didn't want that to happen. She wanted those files to stay open. She wanted Mulder to keep on with his work. And she wanted to help him. She had seen enough to want to see more. Mulder was right about her. She was like him. She was the kind of person who wanted answers. She was the kind of person who *needed* answers—no matter what they turned out to be.

"It's time to tell the truth," Mulder said.

Scully stiffened. Then she realized he wasn't talking to her. He was talking to Theresa.

"You were the one who called me tonight, weren't you, Theresa?" Mulder said. "You were the one who told me Peggy O'Dell had been killed."

His voice was no longer gentle. It was harsh, demanding. He had decided it was time to take off the gloves, Scully thought. He was like an animal smelling blood. Ruthless. Relentless. It was a side of him Scully hadn't seen before. But she wasn't surprised it was there.

Theresa bit her lip, stayed silent. She tried to turn her eyes away from Mulder's. But Mulder's piercing gaze held her like a vise.

"Yes," she said in a weak voice. "It was me."

"How did you know where to call me?" Mulder wanted to know.

"I heard my father say where you were staying," Theresa said.

Scully caught Mulder's eye. She raised her eyebrows. Was Dr. Jay Nemman the firebug? He had acted mad as the devil the day before. But was he that mad?

Mulder gave a slight shrug. He didn't know. Then he turned back to the doctor's daughter. He was going to find out the truth, even if he had to yank it out of Theresa with pliers.

"Who was your father talking to?" Mulder asked. "Who did he tell about the motel?"

"He was talking to Billy's dad," Theresa said.

"Billy? You mean Billy Miles?" said Mulder.

"Yes. Billy is—" Theresa said. She paused. It was hard for her to say the words. Finally she managed to. "Billy's one of us."

"I know that, Theresa," Mulder said. "You're all in this together. The Class of '89. But let's get back to the present. How did you know Peggy was dead?"

"My dad got a phone call," Theresa said. "I heard him asking over the phone, 'Peggy's dead? You sure?'"

"What time was that?" Scully cut in. She wanted to get the time right—to the minute. Tonight minutes meant a lot. Maybe everything.

"Nine o'clock. A couple of minutes after," Theresa said. "I remember my favorite TV show had just come on when the phone rang."

"And what happened then?" Mulder asked. "After you heard your father talking?"

Theresa shook her head helplessly. "I don't know. I can't remember. Next thing I remember, I was in the woods. Someone was chasing me."

"Who?" Mulder said.

"I don't know," the girl said. She seemed near tears again.

But Mulder did not let up. "Was it your father?" he said.

"No," Theresa said. Her voice was barely above a whisper. "But Daddy said never to tell anyone. About any of it."

"You're not supposed to tell anybody about any of *what*?" Mulder demanded sharply.

Scully couldn't blame him. By now she felt the same way he did. They were too close to the truth to let it get away.

"I'm not supposed to tell anyone about Peggy," Theresa said. "Or Billy Miles. Or how Daddy helped."

"Your father helped? Who did he help?" Mulder wanted to know.

"Peggy," Theresa told him.

"How did he help her?" Mulder asked.

"He was Peggy's doctor. She was . . . she was going to have a baby," Theresa said. "But it died."

"Did Billy know about the baby?" Scully asked, beating Mulder to the punch.

"No," Theresa said. "He wasn't around then—he hadn't been for months. He disappeared right before graduation. He didn't come back until almost the end of summer. Peggy said he was the father of her baby. But nobody believed her because he wasn't even here."

"Did your dad know who the father of the baby was?" Mulder asked.

Theresa hesitated again. Then she said, "He helped Peggy. But . . . but there was no baby. There was something else. Daddy said it was because Peggy had the marks."

Scully swallowed hard. She didn't like to think of what Peggy had instead of a baby. But there was no escaping it.

She saw in her mind the remains of the creature they found in the grave.

Her stomach turned over.

She looked at Mulder. He didn't seem bothered. He was leaning forward.

"The marks?" he asked. "You mean the marks on her back?"

"Yes," said Theresa. "We all got them. In the forest. *And we're all going to die.*"

Chapter FIFTEEN

That was as far as Theresa could go.

Now she put her hands over her ears, lay her forehead on the table, and broke into violent sobs.

Scully reached out to touch her hand. It was still icy cold.

Then Theresa raised her head.

"Oh, God," Scully said.

Blood was pouring out of Theresa's nose.

Scully grabbed a handful of paper napkins from a dispenser. She handed them to Theresa.

As she did so, a picture flashed into her mind. The creature in the coffin. The implant in its nostrils.

Was the same implant in Theresa's—?

That was as far as Scully's thinking got.

Out of the corner of her eye, she saw the diner door swing open.

Dr. Jay Nemman stormed into the diner. Close behind him was the police detective from the clearing in the woods. He looked meaner than ever.

The waitress pointed to the table where Scully and Mulder sat with Theresa.

"There's your little girl, Doc," the waitress said.

"Goodness only knows what they've been doing to her, poor thing."

Scully realized the waitress must have made a phone call. Folks around here stuck together—especially when outsiders were concerned.

Outsiders from earth, anyway.

Dr. Nemman ignored Scully and Mulder. He had eyes only for his daughter.

He put his hand on her shoulder. "Let's go home, honey," he said. "You'll be best off there. Away from these prying people and their painful questions."

But Theresa shrank from his touch. Her eyes were wide with terror.

"I don't think the girl wants to leave," Mulder said in a flat voice.

"Now you just stay out of this," the doctor snapped. "She's a sick girl. A very sick girl. She imagines things. All kinds of things. She's on the verge of a mental breakdown. She should not become excited."

By now Theresa had retreated to the corner of the diner booth. She formed her body into a half ball. Like a baby in the womb.

The police detective reached out his arm toward her.

"Your daddy wants to take you home, Theresa, honey," he said soothingly. "He'll get you all cleaned up. Put you to bed. Give you some nice hot chocolate. Now wouldn't that taste good?"

"We're going to take you where you'll be safe, sweetheart," Dr. Nemman chimed in. "You know that Detective Miles and I won't let anything happen to you."

Mulder suddenly sat ramrod straight in his seat.

"You're Billy Miles' father?" he asked the detective.

The big detective turned toward Mulder. "That's right." He looked down at Mulder menacingly. "And you stay away from my boy, hear? Bad enough he's like he is. I don't want outsiders gawking at him like he's something in a zoo."

"Come on, Joe, help me," Dr. Nemman said to Detective Miles.

Nemman took one of Theresa's arms, and Miles took the other. Together they hauled her and half dragged her out of the diner.

Neither Mulder and Scully made a move to stop them. No way they could argue with the rights of a parent and power of the law. Theresa give them one last terrified look as she went out the door.

"You have to love this place," said Mulder, finishing his coffee. "Every day's like Halloween."

"Can we believe a word she said?" Scully said.

"Maybe her father was telling the truth. Maybe she is crazy. This town seems to breed them. Maybe it's something in the diet."

"Do you think anybody, crazy or not, could make all that up?" said Mulder.

"You know the answer to that," Scully said. "But it's still hard to make sense of it. For instance, Peggy O'Dell's watch stopped at three minutes past nine o'clock. That's when she was supposed to have been hit by the train. But Theresa said that Miles told her father about the death just after nine. He couldn't have."

"Who knows?" said Mulder. "She could have been wrong about the time. People make mistakes about things like that. Or she could have been lying. Lying to us—or even to herself. There are things that are hard to admit. Like her having a telepathic connection with Peggy. Those kids in the Class of '89 were linked together by something. Something they couldn't break free of."

Mulder raised his coffee cup to his lips. He realized it was empty.

"Anyway, whatever the truth is, it wouldn't stand up in court," he went on. "Nothing Theresa said would. A girl as upset as she. A girl whose own father says she's unbalanced. No court would take her word against a doctor's. Or a cop's."

Scully nodded. "Imagine you describing what

happened on the highway where X marked the spot. At three minutes after nine o'clock, when you said time took a three-minute holiday. I won't say it did or it didn't. But for sure don't try telling it to a judge."

Mulder smiled bitterly. "I've long since stopped trying to tell things to judges. What you need is hard evidence."

"You're not the only one who knows that," Scully said. "Whoever wrecked the coronor's office and torched our motel rooms knew it, too. All we have to show for our work is ashes."

"Who do you think the firebug is?" said Mulder. "The good Doctor Nemman?"

"Could be," said Scully, thinking hard. "He's not exactly our pal. Maybe Billy's father was working with him. I can see both of them against us. Both of them covering somebody's tracks."

Suddenly Mulder stood up from his seat.

By now Scully recognized the signs.

She got up, too.

"Where to now?" she asked.

"It just hit me," Mulder said. "There still may be some evidence they haven't destroyed."

"Where?" Scully said.

But Mulder was heading for the door.

Scully raced after him to the car. He beat her to the driver's seat.

"Careful," she told Mulder as they raced down the road. It had clouded over again. A fine rain was falling. The asphalt was slick. "We won't solve this case if we're corpses."

"At least we'd wind up in the right place," said Mulder. He kept the accelerator down to the floorboard.

Finally the car braked to a sharp stop. Scully peered out. They were at the edge of Bellefleur Hillside Cemetery.

Mulder got out, and so did Scully. Mulder turned on his flashlight. Then he led the way over the wet grass and muddy soil.

He stopped.

"Too late," he said.

His flashlight played over two opened graves. Beside them were two coffins with their lids off.

Mulder shone his flashlight into them.

Scully looked over his shoulder.

"Both empty," Mulder said. "I should have known."

"What's going on here?" asked Scully. "Is everything in this case crazy? Or are we the crazy ones?"

Mulder wasn't listening.

He stood there, his face vacant, off in a world of his own.

All Scully could do was wait.

Slowly life came back to his face.

He took Scully by the shoulders. His eyes were shining brightly. It was the light of pure joy.

His voice was lit with the same joy.

"It just came to me," he told her. "I know who it is."

"Who *who* is?" said Scully.

"Who did it," said Mulder.

"Did it?" Scully said. "You mean, killed Peggy?"

Mulder nodded happily.

"And the rest?" said Scully. "Stole our evidence? Scared Theresa out of her wits? The same person?"

Mulder kept nodding.

"One and the same," he said. "I know who it is."

Chapter SIXTEEN

"I hate to spoil your fun—but I think I already know the answer," said Scully. She had been putting a lot of pieces together in her mind. She thought she had the puzzle solved.

"Do you?" said Mulder. "Do you really?"

"Is it the big cop—Detective Miles?"

"Good try," said Mulder. "You're a credit to the Academy. But—no."

"No?" said Scully.

"No—but you're close," said Mulder.

"Close?" said Scully.

"It's his son—Billy Miles," Mulder declared.

Scully could see that Mulder might be a nice guy. Well-meaning. Talented. With his heart in the right place.

But his head was definitely screwed on wrong.

She smiled at him as she shook her head.

"Billy Miles?" she said. "You mean the kid who's been a vegetable for the last four years? He got out here and dug up these graves all by himself?"

Mulder nodded.

"I don't know if I completely understand it," he told Scully. "All the details. But it fits a profile of alien abduction. Believe me, I know what I'm talking about. I've run hundreds of cases through a computer and—"

"*This* fits a *profile?*" said Scully. She thought of the total insanity of the past couple of days. Some profile that must be.

"Listen," Mulder said. "Peggy O'Dell's watch stopped at three minutes after nine o'clock. You saw it. That's exactly when we lost three minutes out on the highway. Meanwhile, at the same time, Theresa Nemman somehow left her house and wound up running for her life in the woods. I think something happened in those three minutes. When time as we know it stopped."

"Sure, Mulder, sure," Scully said. "Now why don't we go back to the motel. You can have a nice glass of hot milk. Get a good night's sleep. You'll feel better in the morning."

Mulder raised his eyebrows.

"You don't believe me?" he said.

"Agent Mulder, I'm standing out in the mud and drizzle," said Scully. "I'm looking at two empty coffins. I'm in a cemetery where we dug up someone or something I can't explain. Meanwhile, a whacked-out kid just told me she's going to die because she has 'the marks.' Sure, I believe you, Mulder. But that doesn't mean you're right. It means I'm going around the bend myself. At this point, I'd believe

anyone or anything. It wouldn't surprise me if we
both started howling at the moon."

"Calm down, Scully, and listen," Mulder told her.

"Calm down?" said Scully. "I'd need a couple of
good strong pills for that."

But strangely enough, she did feel herself calm-
ing down. Maybe it was something in Mulder's
voice. His passion for the truth. His complete con-
viction. Whatever it was, she shut up and listened.

"I think there's a force at work here in
Bellefleur," Mulder told her. "We felt it on the plane
just before we landed. We experienced it out on the
highway. There was a strange force at work there.
Our watches played tricks. My compass went hay-
wire. What I'm saying is—I think this force can
bend time. So that Billy Miles could go dig up these
graves. And loot. And burn. And kill. With no one
around to see that he was gone from his bed."

Scully told herself not to listen to Mulder. But it
was like being in the water and fighting an under-
tow. She felt the pull of his thinking—its power and
its purpose. She was losing her footing, being pulled
farther and farther out to sea.

"This 'force'—it expands time?" she heard herself asking.

"Yes," he answered. "And it's what caused the
marks on those kids' backs. The kids with the
marks have been abducted and used in tests.

They're taken to that clearing in the woods. The substance we can't identify is put into their bodies. It causes a genetic mutation."

"So this 'force' was chasing Theresa through the woods tonight?"

"No," said Mulder. "It was Billy Miles. He was acting from an impulse implanted in his DNA. Danny Doty feels the same kind of impulses in his genes. That's why he wants to stay in prison. He knows he can't obey them if he's behind bars."

Scully nodded. Of course. It made sense. Complete sense. No question about it. Mulder was perfectly sane in telling her all this. And she was perfectly sane in listening to it and nodding and urging him to tell her more. It was the rest of the world that was—

She doubled over as a wave of laughter hit her.

Mulder looked at her and started laughing, too.

They stood there in the cemetery in the darkness and the drizzle, laughing their heads off.

"You know, we're crazy," Scully finally said.

"Of course we are," Mulder gasped out.

At last he caught his breath.

"Come on," he told Scully. "Let's go."

"Where are we going?" asked Scully, still feeling weak with laughter.

"Where we belong," said Mulder. "To the funny farm. To see Billy Miles."

Chapter SEVENTEEN

Scully stood with Mulder at Billy Miles' bedside. The orderly who took care of Billy was there as well.

"We can wait 'til the second coming for Billy to get out of this bed," the orderly told them. "It ain't gonna happen."

Billy lay there, quiet as a corpse. Only the smallest rise and fall of his chest showed he was breathing. His face looked like a death mask. His eyes were blank as glass.

"Three years he's been lying here like this," the orderly said. "And a year before that at home."

"You're sure?" Scully asked. "He never makes a move?"

"I keep a close eye on him," the orderly assured her. "His old man, he pays me extra to do that. He made me swear that if there's any sign of life, I tell him first. Believe me, Billy even blinks, and I know it."

Mulder had been listening. Now he stepped forward and took over. "Did you change his bedpan last night?"

"Nobody else here gonna do it," the orderly said.

"You notice anything unusual?" Mulder asked.

"Unusual?" said the orderly, puzzled. "What you mean? What kind of unusual thing could happen here with Billy? Like I already told you, he hasn't moved in—"

"What were you doing last night at nine o'clock?" Mulder cut in.

"Probably watching TV," said the orderly. "Yeah. Sure. That's right. I was watching the tube."

"What were you watching?" Mulder asked sharply.

"Sure. It was . . . it was . . ." The orderly paused. He was suddenly confused. "Funny about that, I can't exactly remember what—"

He stopped abruptly. Scully was leaning over Billy's bed.

She had spotted something. A black smudge on Billy's clean white sheets. She moved to the foot of the bed. She started pulling at the blanket.

"Hey, what are you doing?" the orderly wanted to know.

Scully paid no attention to him. She pulled the blanket free and looked down at Billy's bare feet.

"What you looking for?" the orderly demanded.

Scully found what she was looking for under a toenail. Dirt. Black dirt.

The orderly was angry. He didn't like this stranger meddling with Billy. Billy was his job. More than his job. His meal ticket.

The orderly opened his mouth to shoo Scully off. Before he could, Mulder shot him another question. "Who was taking care of Peggy O'Dell last night?"

"Not me," the orderly defended himself. "That's not my ward. Not my part of the vegetable garden. It's a shame about that girl, though. She sure enough liked Billy here. I think she did him more good than all them doctors. I sometimes even thought Billy actually kind of knew she was there."

"How could she have gotten out of here?" Mulder asked. "Without her wheelchair?"

"I don't know," the orderly insisted. "Like I said, that's not my thing."

Then he noticed Scully again. She had taken a metal instrument out of her purse. She used it to scrape dirt from under Billy's toenails. She put it in a small glass vial. She finished the job before the orderly could tell her to stop.

All the orderly could do was ask, "What the devil you want to do that for?"

Mulder answered for Scully. "Thank you for your time," he said.

The orderly was left openmouthed as Mulder and Scully made their exit.

The orderly was back to having only Billy to talk to. He didn't mind, though. He was used to it. He talked to Billy every working day. It didn't bother him that the conversation was so one-sided. The orderly liked the sound of his own voice.

"Now look what that girl did," the orderly said. "Messed up the nice hospital corners of these sheets. Gotta fix them again. 'Course, she did give your nails a nice cleaning, though how they got so dirty I don't know. Guess you must sweat or something. I mean, you are alive, Billy boy. Else your old man wouldn't give me that little bonus every week. Still, I earn my pay. No fun being cooped up with you all the time. I mean, you ain't my dream companion. Besides which, I think it's affecting my mind. I could have sworn you actually gave that girl a look when she scraped your nails. Which means I'd better take some time off this job. Else soon somebody's gonna be looking after *me*."

Meanwhile, outside, Scully was saying to Mulder, "Guess where I want to go now?"

"It'll just take twenty minutes to drive back to the motel—or what's left of it," Mulder said.

"Then I guess I don't have to tell you what we're looking for," Scully said.

"Let's hope we can find it," Mulder said.

Scully wrinkled up her nose as they went through the charred remains of her motel room. Fire left an awful stink. But a second later she forgot the smell.

"We're in luck," she told Mulder, picking up a half melted baggy. Its contents were intact. "I knew I was right taking a sample from the forest clearing."

"Score one for your Academy training," Mulder agreed.

"Here's something else that survived, too," she said. She picked up a glass vial. It had cracked, but the tiny metal implant—the implant from the creature in the coffin—was still inside.

"Our firebug friend might be good—but he's not *that* good," Scully said.

"Time to see how good we are," said Mulder. "Let's get to the lab. There's work to do."

"No sweat," Scully assured him. "It'll be child's play."

She was right. The job was a snap. She put the dirt from under Billy's toenail on a glass slide. Beside it she put the sample from the forest clearing. Once the slide was under a microscope, she needed only a quick look.

"We've hit pay dirt," she announced. "They're a perfect match."

"Put 'er there, partner," Mulder exulted. His palm went up to slap Scully's in a stinging high-five. "Goal to go!"

Chapter EIGHTEEN

"Looks like we're not alone," Mulder said.

Their car headlights lit up a four-wheel-drive truck. It was parked at the forest edge.

Scully recognized it right away. "Our old pal, Detective Miles," she said. "He sure does like these woods at night."

"Must be a boy scout who never grew up," Mulder said. "Wonder what good deed he's planning tonight."

"I'm sure we'll find out," Scully said. "But let's not worry about it now. There's more to find out first."

She parked the car beside the truck. They got out and lit their flashlights. They followed the bright beams through the dark trees.

"You'd think we'd know our way by now," Scully said. "But in these woods, I always feel a little lost. Or maybe it's not these woods. Maybe it's this whole case. I keep losing my bearings. Every time we find one answer, a new question pops up."

"Welcome to the club," Mulder said, brushing aside a branch. "I've felt that way for years now. It's like being in a maze. A maze with endless twists and turns. A maze built to confound you no matter how smart you think you are."

He fell silent. There were only the night sounds of the forest. The wind in the trees. An owl hooting. The scurrying of unknown animals. And the soft crunching of their footsteps on fallen leaves.

Then Mulder said, "What about you, Scully? What do you think about this maze? Does it spook you? Does it make you want to turn tail and get out while the getting's good? Or are you like me? Have you gotten in too deep to turn back?"

"Do I have to answer that question right now?" she asked, half joking. "Or am I allowed to consult my notes?"

"Take all the time you want," Mulder said. "But you'll have to give the answer sometime, you know. Not to me. To yourself. And of course to the folks who sent you into this with me. Our dear bosses."

"I'll worry about that later," Scully said. She found the spot where she had scooped the gray ashes and black earth. "Look," she said. Her light shone on imprints in the ashes.

"Footprints," said Mulder.

"Bare footprints," Scully said. "It figures."

"Listen," Mulder said. "Someone's running."

Scully heard it, too. The sound of a body crashing through the underbrush.

Mulder swung his flashlight toward the sound. He was fast enough to spot a figure moving into the trees. But he wasn't fast enough to see who it was.

Scully watched Mulder take off. She hesitated for one violent heartbeat. Then she broke into a run. Maybe she couldn't catch up with him. But she wanted to keep him in sight.

Scully was a Redskin fan. Now she knew what it was like to follow a zigzagging blocker on a broken field run. Mulder darted in and out of the trees ahead of her. Scully tried not to lose him. For a second she was sure she had. Then she saw him through a break in the trees. He was drawing away from her. She had to speed up. Her legs felt like lead weights. Her breath ripped at her lungs. But she made herself breathe deeper, move faster—

Blatt.

Something hit the back of her legs very hard.

Suddenly her legs were no longer under her.

She was falling.

She felt the impact to her elbows as she hit the ground palms first.

Her chin was resting on the ground. She slowly lifted her head. She stared at a pair of scuffed and dirt-covered boots.

Her eyes traveled upward over massive legs in dark blue pants. Next she saw a big stomach straining shirt buttons as it hung over a taut belt. Then her gaze fastened on a gleaming shotgun pointed at her head.

She didn't have to bother checking out the man's face. "Detective Miles," she said. "Fancy running into you here."

"Touch my kid and I'll kill you," he promised.

Then he was off and running.

Scully knew where Miles was going. But maybe she could catch up with Mulder before the kill-crazy cop did. She didn't know what she could do to help him. But there had to be something. Anything. How she wished she had her gun. Or that Mulder had his. Karate was fine. But even a black belt couldn't beat a bullet.

She picked herself up and raced through the woods. But now she was running blind. She had lost sight of both Mulder and Miles. All she could do was run and hope and pray she got to Mulder in time.

Then she was at the edge of another clearing. Her heart skipped a beat. She saw Mulder.

He was standing on the far side of the clearing, shining his flashlight at the center of the open space.

There, frozen in the beam of light, was Billy Miles standing in his pajama bottoms.

Scully gripped a tree trunk to steady herself.

She could see two red marks on Billy's back.

Seeing them shook her up enough. But the limp figure cradled in Billy's arms shook her up even more.

It was Theresa Nemman. The doctor's daughter was in her nightgown and bathrobe. She was dead to the world.

"Billy!" Mulder shouted. "Put her down, Billy!"

Billy looked at Mulder blankly. He might have been on a different planet.

Then it was Scully's turn to shout.

She saw Detective Miles coming out from the trees behind Mulder. He had his shotgun at the ready. And he had murder in his eyes.

"Mulder!" Scully screamed out at the top of her aching lungs. "Look out! Behind you! He's got a gun! He's going to—!"

But even as the words left her mouth, she knew they were too late.

Chapter NINETEEN

Mulder heard Scully's shout. He had time to turn around. He had time to see Miles charging out of the forest. But there was no time to stop Miles from gunning him down.

But the big detective didn't even seem to see Mulder.

He had eyes only for his boy.

"Billy! I love you! But this is the only way!" Miles roared like a wounded grizzly—and raised his gun.

It went off—up into the air.

Miles had gone down—hit by Mulder's tackle.

The Redskins could use this guy, thought Scully.

She saw Mulder bending to grab the shotgun. She started forward to help him. Meanwhile, Billy stayed frozen, with Theresa in his arms. He looked like an incredibly lifelike statue.

Then Scully froze, as the clearing came to life.

A twister of dust and leaves swirled up from the ground. It formed a whirling wall around Billy and his burden. Wind howled through the trees. Above the wind a humming rose. Behind the humming, a clanging began. And with the clanging, dazzling white light flooded the clearing. Mulder and Miles vanished in the blinding blaze.

It ended as suddenly as it began.

Scully blinked, trying to focus. She saw Billy and the girl side by side on the ground. They were covered by fallen dust and leaves.

Mulder and Miles saw them, too. The two men got to their feet and ran to the fallen pair. Scully arrived at the same time they did.

Miles knelt beside his son.

"Billy," he said in a choked voice.

Billy raised his head. "Dad . . . ?" he managed to say. He rose to his feet, his father helping him. Beside him, Theresa stirred. Scully helped her get up.

"Who are you?" the girl said. "What am I doing here?"

Scully looked into the girl's dazed eyes. Then she felt a hand on her arm. It was Mulder. She followed his silent gaze. He was looking at Billy's back. Scully had to stifle a cry.

The red marks were gone.

"Detective Miles," Mulder said, "you don't mind if we ask Billy a few questions."

"Mind? No. Not at all," the detective said. He held Billy in a gentle bear hug. He was looking at his son with wonder and joy. "You kept me from doing the craziest thing a father could ever do. You saved my boy's life. You helped bring him back from the dead. Anything you want is okay by me."

The detective insisted on driving Billy back to the mental hospital himself. Mulder and Scully dropped Theresa off at her home. Then they headed for the hospital.

"Hey, slow down," Mulder cautioned Scully. "We both can't be reckless drivers."

"How true," said Scully. She reluctantly slowed the car to the legal speed limit. Mulder was right. She didn't want to crash—not before they got their answers from Billy.

Billy was back in his bed when they arrived. Dr. Glass was with him. The psychiatrist looked puzzled.

"A most unusual case," he said. "In all my years, I've never seen anything like it."

"You're right," Mulder said. "It is a most unusual case. That's why it's important we question Billy."

"Of course," Dr. Glass agreed. "But keep the session short. He's still weak. Recovery will take a while."

Billy did look weak, lying in the bed he had lain in for three years. But his eyes were alive now. And though his voice was faint, it was clear.

Mulder kept his own voice low-pitched. He did not want to disturb Billy's mental balance. It was still as fragile as a house of cards.

"Tell me about that light, Billy," Mulder said. "When did you first see it?"

"In the forest," Billy said. "We were all in the forest. We were having a party. All my friends. We were celebrating."

"What were you celebrating?" Mulder asked.

"Graduation," Billy said.

"But you never graduated," Mulder said.

"No," said Billy. "The light took me away."

"Where did it take you?" Mulder asked.

"To the testing place," Billy explained.

"Did they do tests on you?" Mulder asked.

"Yes," Billy said.

"Did you help them test the others?" Mulder asked.

"Yes," Billy said. "I would wait for their orders. To gather the others."

"How did they give the orders?" Mulder asked.

"Through the implant," Billy said. "But the tests didn't work. I—"

Billy's voice was wavering now. It was like a candle flame flickering in a breeze.

"You what?" Mulder urged him to try to answer. Mulder leaned forward to catch his words. Behind Mulder, Scully did the same.

They saw tears rolling down Billy's cheeks. They heard Billy say between sobs, "They said it would be okay. They didn't want anyone to know. They wanted everything destroyed. I'm afraid. Afraid they're coming back."

"Nothing to be afraid of," Mulder tried to assure him. "Now if you can just tell me—"

But Billy had said everything he was going to that night. He was weeping uncontrollably.

"I'm afraid that has to be all," Dr. Glass told Mulder. "I hope you've heard enough."

"Don't ask me," Mulder told him. "Ask Agent Scully here."

But Mulder did it himself. "What about it, Scully," he asked her. "You heard enough? Enough for your report?"

Chapter **TWENTY**

"They're waiting for you," Special Agent Jones told Scully.

Scully almost turned to exchange looks with Mulder. But she didn't. Because Mulder wasn't there.

Funny, she thought, how she had gotten used to Mulder being around. Funny how fast they had turned into a team.

She was alone now, though. Back at F.B.I. Headquarters in Washington. The big brass had read the report she turned in. Now they wanted to see her.

Jones led her into the conference room. She saw the same men around the table as before.

Did she look the same to them? The same sound and sane agent they had put on a crackpot's case?

She tried to look like her old cool, imposed self as she sat down. Then, she waited for the questions to begin.

The elderly man who was top gun was the first to speak.

"We've been going over your report, Ms. Scully," he said. "Frankly, we don't know what to make of it."

The man next to him demanded, "Did Agent

Mulder try to trick you in some way? Throw dust in your eyes? Brainwash you?"

Scully answered firmly. "No, sir. Agent Mulder allowed me to make up my own mind. No smoke. No mirrors. Fair and square."

A third man joined in. His voice had a nasty edge. "So you think we have space aliens flying around America? Zapping people with ray guns?"

Scully forced a polite smile. She acted as if he were making a little joke. "No, sir," she answered. "I don't think we have enough evidence to say that. Not for sure."

"I've read about the evidence you do have," the second speaker growled. "Time warps. Grotesque corpses. And what about that other thing? What you call an implant?"

Scully pulled a glass vial from her pocket. Maybe it would do what her report clearly had not. Maybe these men would believe their own eyes.

The men passed the vial from hand to hand. Each in turn squinted at the metal object inside.

"Our lab tests could not identify the metal," Scully told them. "This came from the corpse's nasal cavity. Billy Miles described the same object. He said it was in his nose, too. It told him to kill. You could call it a kind of fax—used to deliver a message of murder."

The vial rested in the top man's hand. He stared at it, trying to think what he could say about it.

In the end, he could only look at Scully hard and say, "Let's get back to earth. What's happened to the boy? Billy? Are they putting him on trial?"

"They've decided that Billy's father and the county medical examiner obstructed justice," said Scully. "Billy, of course, has confessed his part in the deaths."

"His *part*?" exclaimed the second speaker. "Who else could be involved?"

Before Scully could answer, the top man demanded, "Are you saying the boy will be put on trial for murder?"

"No, sir," Scully said. "We persuaded the local law to drop the case. We said it would be best for all concerned."

"Darn right," the second speaker declared. "That's all we need. A slick lawyer putting Mulder on the stand. Using an F.B.I. agent to beat a murder rap with an 'alien abduction' defense."

The third speaker asked Scully sharply, "Did anyone stop to think that the boy might just be an insanely clever killer?"

Scully fumbled for an answer she didn't have. But the top man saved her from having to pull a rabbit out of a hat.

"Let's get back to the point of this meeting," he said. "What does Agent Mulder believe?"

Now Scully faced another problem. There was too much she could say. Too much that Mulder had revealed to her. Too much that almost nobody else in the world would believe.

Certainly not the men waiting for her answer.

She did the best she could. She said the least she could.

"Agent Mulder thinks we are not alone."

The top man gave her a long hard look. Then he made a tiny movement of his shoulders. It just might have been a shrug.

"Thank you, Ms. Scully," he said. "You may go."

"I just want to say that—" Scully began.

"Thank you, Ms. Scully," the man repeated.

"Yes, sir. Thank you, sir," Scully said.

Her stomach was sinking as she got to her feet.

Only one thing stopped it from sinking still more. The small smile that Agent Jones gave her as he let her out the door. That smile seemed to say that she had done just fine.

Jones's smile faded as he closed the door from the inside. His face was deadpan as he went back to join his bosses.

The men at the table were busy comparing notes.

"Her report is a match with those classified

Pentagon papers," the third speaker said. He shook his head.

The second speaker shared his concern. "It would be murder if this got to the press. Or if Congress got hold of it. We'd have to spend all our time chasing ghosts and spacemen."

A previously silent man said sourly, "F.B.I. would stand for Federal Boogeymen Investigators."

"It would cause mass hysteria," the third speaker declared.

The top man listened quietly until they were finished. All eyes turned to him, waiting for his decision.

He cleared his throat.

"Gentlemen," he said. "This report offers no hard evidence. We will have to let Agent Scully keep her eye on Mulder. She must give us enough facts to close the X-files for good. Until then, the information in Agent Scully's report will not leave this room. Special Agent Jones, file the evidence in the usual manner."

"Yes, sir," Jones said.

He collected all copies of the report from the table. They made a thick stack. Scully had done a thorough job.

Then the head man handed him the glass vial with the metal implant.

"Take special care of this," he told Jones.

"Yes, sir," Jones said.

Jones first stop was in the basement of Bureau headquarters. He let himself into a room that few agents knew about. And to which even fewer had a key.

Inside was a a stainless steel furnace. He opened its door and tossed in the reports. He pressed a button. He watched orange flames leap up hungrily.

He waited until the fire did its job. Then he left, walking quickly.

He went to the Headquarters parking lot.

"I need a Bureau car," he told the attendant.

"Another special assignment, Jones?" the man said. "Nice day for a drive. Some guys get all the luck. Me, I have to stay on post 'til six."

"Yeah, lucky me," Jones said.

He left the city. He crossed the Potomac and drove through the green Virginia countryside. He turned off the highway down a narrow unmarked blacktop.

He stopped before iron gates in a high stone wall. It looked like the entrance to a private estate. But private estates did not have two soldiers with semiautomatics on guard.

"Hi, Jones," said the sergeant in charge as Jones flashed his ID. "Another job?"

"Another job," agreed Jones.

The gates swung open, and Jones followed the blacktop to a huge, square, windowless concrete building.

Jones showed his ID to the soldier at the door and entered.

The inside was a maze of floor-to-ceiling shelves. They were crammed with steel boxes, all locked.

Jones did not pause. He knew exactly where he was going.

At the far end of the warehouse he stopped. He took out a key and opened a steel box marked with a code number.

He carefully placed the glass vial inside.

Right next to four other identical glass vials.

As he closed and locked the box, he wondered how many more trips he would have to make.

He thought of Scully. He thought of Mulder. He thought of the X-files overflowing with cases.

As he left the building, he said to the guard, "Be seeing you."